The Christmas Wife

A list of books in the series appears at the end of this volume.

THE CHRISTMAS WIFE

Stories by
Helen Norris

UNIVERSITY OF ILLINOIS PRESS

Urbana and Chicago

Short Story Index
84-88

For Carolyn

*Publication of this work was supported in part
by grants from the National Endowment for the Arts
and the Illinois Arts Council, a state agency.*

©1985 by Helen Norris
Manufactured in the United States of America
C 5 4 3 2 1

This book is printed on acid-free paper.

"The Love Child," *Sewanee Review* 91, no. 2 (Spring 1983); reprinted in
  Prize Stories, 1984: The O. Henry Awards
"The Quarry," *Stories* #7 (September 1983); reprinted in *Prize Stories, 1985:
  The O. Henry Awards*
"The Christmas Wife," *Sun Dog* 4, no. 2 (Fall 1982); reprinted in *Stories,*
  August 1983
"The Singing Well," *TriQuarterly* (forthcoming)
"Money Man," *Sun Dog* 4, no. 1 (Spring 1982)
"The Healing," *New England Review and Bread Loaf Quarterly* 5, no. 4
  (Summer 1983)

Library of Congress Cataloging in Publication Data

Norris, Helen, 1916–
  The Christmas wife.

  (Illinois short fiction)
  I. Title.
PS 3527.0497C4   1985   813'.52   84-24080
ISBN 0-252-01206-2 (alk. paper)

Contents

The Love Child

The wind was brawling out of the north when they told her she had to move. Her son Sam, who was getting gray and stout, and his tall wife Ardis, who dyed her hair the color of peanut brittle, came down from Memphis to tell her, leaving their children with a neighbor overnight.

She was seventy-six. She had lived in her house for fifty years and she refused to leave.

"Mama, they're going to put a highway clean through your house. You wouldn't like that, Mama. Would you want the cars running straight through your living room?"

"Yes," Emma said. She was always difficult when they talked to her like a child. Then she said, "I never gave my consent. They couldn't do it without my consent."

"Mama, they can. How could you live all your life and not know that? The government can do anything it wants."

So they moved her to a little farmhouse on the outskirts of the town. They bought it for her with the money the government gave them for her own house in town. And they added some, or so Sam said. Because this house was better built and would last for years. "I don't need one that will last," she said. But they didn't listen. It had ten acres of land that stretched back from the road, with a lot of underbrush that needed clearing and trees and a pond with fish that moved like shadows through the feathers of green scum.

"I don't need all this," she said, looking at it from the back porch with her head wrapped in a brown scarf.

"You'll get used to it, Mama. It's a good investment."

She knew they meant that when she died they could sell it at a profit. They expected her to die, she thought. And very soon. But if she thought that, she was wrong: She found they were expecting her to live. After all the work of birthing, raising, nursing, grieving, they wanted one thing more.

Meanwhile in the new place she lasted out the winter, beat it down into the ground. Actually it seemed to disappear into the trees and lie in wait on the other side of the hill. Oh, she hated winter, always had. But it was better in the town, with Mrs. Ellis coming in for coffee. And Mr. Greer, the postman, stamping through the slush and ringing her bell. And the boy from the grocery blowing into his hands, Effie Higgins's boy . . . The days were draughty, noisy with the wind, but they were full of faces she could wave to from her window if she felt like waving. You get older and the world is changing and you hardly know yourself except for people who have always known you and you can see it in their faces who you are. Then you know.

Here the days were long and soaked with rain and all her past, and no one was coming in or passing by. Even the rain was different, blowing now from the left instead of the right. She took off her steel-rimmed glasses and stared at her face, all blurry, in the mirror. It's what I'm like inside, she said. I don't know who I am. I'm blurred inside.

But the spring brought Sam and Ardis. They had called the night before. She watched them drive up and get out. They had with them one of their three children, who was staying in the back seat of the car. She saw her grandchildren so seldom that she wasn't sure which one it was.

"Is that Todd or Steven? Bring him in. Or show him the pond in back."

They looked at one another. "Mama, we have to talk to you first." And they followed her in and got right to the point. "Mama, it isn't . . . Mama, it's Cissie's child."

Cissie was her grandchild, the daughter of her own child Rachel, who had died a dozen years before.

"Cissie?" she said. "Cissie had a child? I never heard a word of Cissie's wedding."

"Mama, there wasn't any wedding. She was fifteen and she ran off. We took her in when Rachel died and did the best we could. You know we did. We raised her like our own."

"Cissie ran away and had a child? At fifteen?" She was trying to see the polished skin, the green eyes, the fluffy hair of Cissie. "Why are you telling me this now? I can't help what she did. Young people now, they're not the way we were."

"We didn't want to worry you, because we didn't know where she was. And then she came back, and she brought this child . . ." They were looking through the window at the pond. "We've kept him through the winter. But we have our own."

Her voice was full of wonder. "Why isn't Cissie keeping him?"

"Mama, Cissie's found a man who wants to marry her. She wants to start all over. We can all see that's the best . . . But we have our own three children. Mama, we've brought him here."

After a while she asked, "You've brought him here to stay? For how long, Sam?"

"Oh, a while. Just a while." By the way he said it she knew it was forever, for the rest of her days.

"I'm too old," she said. "I'm seventy-six."

"He'll be good for you, Mama. Give you something to live for."

"You mean to die for. I'm too old," she said again. And her age loomed dark before her like a tunnel through the mountain. Their faces were strangers' faces. "I'm not the same," she said. "When your father died . . ."

"Mama, that was eighteen years ago. And you have your health."

"Something broke . . ."

"Mama, it's been eighteen years, and life goes on."

"Mine didn't." She was being difficult again. But when she was difficult they looked at her as if they knew who she was. And then she knew herself.

They stood up, and Ardis stayed with her while Sam went to the car and brought the child. He was very small, with Cissie's fluffy hair and ice-green eyes. He looked up at her for the merest flash of time and then away.

"Ethan," Ardis said, "this is your own great-granny. Uncle Sam was her little boy."

Sam said, "He knows he's staying."

Her voice fought through the tunnel of her age. "How old is he?"

"He's four . . . " His voice was lowered. "Cissie says he was born July the ninth. You might want to do a little something. We'll send a box."

Then Sam got the suitcase with his clothes and a small box with his toys. And they were gone, their Buick eating through the new oak leaves and out into the warm spring sun and down the road.

He was still looking through the window long after they had disappeared. She sat down in a chair and stared at his back in a green striped T-shirt that all but covered his short pants. He was so still and small that she could almost believe he wasn't there. She was dazed and weary. She was trying to think about him and where she would put him and what she would fix for him to eat today and tomorrow and all the days of her life. She thought of all the questions she should have asked Sam.

And so she was given Cissie's love child, as her grandmother would have called him, to have and to hold. The black woman who came to work for them a thousand years ago on the farm where she was born would have said Cissie "found" him.

It was all the same. However made or found, he was given her to keep. So she kept the child. But the strange and chilling fact of their life was that he never looked at her and never spoke. At first she thought him shy, so she talked in a soothing voice of her children when they were young—Sam and Jamie and Rachel—and of her own childhood. He gave no sign of hearing. He sat or stood with vacant eyes on the floor or on the trees and sky or on his brown hands, which were peppered with small warts. She took one of his hands in her own. He did not draw away. "My brother used to have some little lumps like these. I made them go away. Would you let me try to make yours go away?" Slowly, almost absently, he drew his hand from hers.

He ran and played in the yard, but when she was near he seemed to move in his sleep. He did as he was bidden. He went to bed when he was told. He ate what she cooked for him. She tried to win him round with her baking, which she had almost forgotten how to do. He ate the sweet muffins and the cookies silently, then walked away.

He was smaller than he should be for his age, she thought. Cissie had been small. His skin was fair, a little freckled, his nose always pink and peeling from the sun. His hands brown and dotted with the colonies of warts. A rim of insect bites just below his short pants. His hair was pale silk, like Cissie's hair, with bits of leaf or a feather clinging. But his eyes were really not Cissie's at all. They were more like the water at the edge of the pond, gray shading into green and back into gray. But not like the water, for if you looked into them you didn't see yourself. You were never there. Sometimes there was a flicker that moved out of sight, like the fish in the pond that were always just leaving wherever they had been. He was as tight as a nut inside a hard shell. He never came out. He never let her in.

At first she was a little amused at his tightness, then a little dismayed. And then there was a cold hard stone in the center of her breast. Like a question it was. Perhaps it was fear.

To put away the fear or whatever it was, she took to singing to him in her low rusty voice the songs of her childhood about animals and games. When she sang he grew still as a rock, and sometimes his eyes swept in passing her hands or her dress. But never her face. She began to feel faceless. So as not to feel voiceless she needed to talk to him. She needed to sing. And she watched for the slightest sign that he attended to anything at all except a request to go to bed or to eat, to go out or come in, to dress himself or wash . . . When she made a request a kind of pale hardness, translucent like porcelain, would appear in his face. His mouth would move slightly as he pulled on his lip. He seemed to be asleep. But he always obeyed.

Soon after his coming she took his toys from the box and arranged them on top of the cedar chest below the window in the room she had given him. Some of them were toys he must have had since he was very young: a small brown bear with one green eye. A cord with colored spools. A yellow truck. A dozen blocks. A plastic duck. Some soldiers still attached with wire to the card on which they came. A box of crayons. A picture book to color. She placed them in a row on the chest. Then she put his clothes from the suitcase in the chest of drawers.

When she passed his room next, she saw that the toys were back inside the box and the clothes were in the suitcase. She left them there.

The strangest thing of all was that she never heard his voice. Sometimes at night she awoke and thought that he had called. She lay still and listened. She had only dreamed his voice. It was strong and high-pitched. It was Jamie's voice. Even when awake, she thought of Jamie as little, because she had never seen him growing old, getting gray like Sam.

She tried not to think. She unpacked her boxes full of things from the old house. A lot of them were strange to her away from their places on the tables and shelves. She couldn't recall the flowered china bowl. Where did she get it? Where had she kept it? She went on with the unpacking as if she hoped to find herself wrapped in old paper in one of the boxes.

She came across two small harmonicas, both a little rusted, that had belonged to Sam and Jamie. She tried them out in secret, and then she placed one in the pocket of her apron and one on the table in the dining room. In a day or two she heard what she was waiting for. When she was in the kitchen there came the voice of the harmonica — one note sustained, a long pause, and then the same note three times. She took the mate from her pocket and blew an answer. She held her breath to listen. There was nothing. After a moment she looked into the dining room. He was gone and the harmonica was on the table where she had placed it. She grew to believe that she had dreamt its sound.

She tried to read the magazines that came in the mail, but words meant nothing any more. Words got in her way. Sometimes she stroked the dried-out skin of her arms with the coarsely woven cloth of her long cotton sleeves. Or she held her face with both hands. Or she moved her legs deliberately when she walked across the room. Or she drank the well water that tasted of moss, holding it in her mouth till it slid down her throat and into her bones and she shuddered with the cold. I'm here. I'm alive.

But the trees outside were more alive and full of growth, their balled leaves bursting into hands and fingers. The weeds and grass shot up around her porch, crowding the steps as if they wanted to come in. At night the long tendrils of wisteria were scratching at her window — all of it alive, more alive than herself. All of it knowing itself and who it was. She was canceled by the spring. It was worse than the winter.

She might have willed herself into the world if only Ethan had known her.

She waited one night till Ethan went to bed. When she was sure he was asleep she rang up Sam in Memphis. Ardis answered.

"There's something I need to know," she said, "about the boy . . ." She could feel that Ardis was waiting, tapping her long teeth with the nail of one finger as she liked to do. "Can he talk? I mean he hasn't said a word . . ."

"Mama, he's probably shy. When he gets used to you . . ."

"I mean does he know any words?"

"Any what?"

"Any words. Does he know any words?"

There was a silence. She thought she could hear the click of Ardis's teeth.

"Mama, he's almost five. Let me put it this way: he knows as many words as Steve and Todd."

She waited for a moment, enduring the impatience at the end of the line. "Tell Sam I called."

She thought more and more about her house in town. She dreamt of it at night. And in her dreams she walked from room to room touching the things that had made her who she was — the fireplace, the mantel, the lattice doors, the kitchen windows overlooking the trees, the wall of bricks where the porch had been extended when her husband was alive, the sill where Rachel sat when she painted her pictures of the shed in vivid colors, a different color every time, rusting out the screen where her jar of water spilled. She had never really believed the house would not be there. Or the street with its lacing of sycamore boughs . . .

She put Ethan in the car, the ancient Plymouth that had taken her away from her house, and drove into town and straight to her street. It was indeed gone or soon would be. The bulldozers were prowling the devastation like prehistoric monsters. Her house, when she found it, had gone to rubble, the boards heaped and broken, the chimney crumbled in upon itself, the hearthplace buried.

It was the scattered chimney that broke her heart. She had a strange guilty feeling that if she had not deserted the house it would still be alive.

The child beside her was standing up to look at the machines. "That used to be my house," she said. He gave no sign of hearing. If only she had someone to share it with. Mrs. Ellis had gone away to live with her daughter in another state. Mr. Greer the postman would not be coming round. She did not know about the rest. They seemed to her dead. She went on talking. "Your mother used to come and visit when she was your age. Such a pretty little girl. She always played in the swing . . . "

She gave it up and cried a little. He did not seem to notice. She drove them away. Mrs. Ellis had a niece with a child who couldn't love. She said he couldn't belong to them, only to himself. When Mrs. Ellis talked of him she shook her head from side to side and smoothed the dress on her knee. He would never be right. There was a name for it, but Mrs. Ellis could never remember what it was. She drank a second cup of coffee; still she couldn't remember.

The sun was growing hot. The air was still. For three whole days Emma mourned for the house and for her crumbled life. Tears swam in her eyes, blurred the figure of Ethan and the field that shimmered in the late spring heat, but dried on her lashes before they fell. The tears were a comfort and still they were a shame. They seemed to be tears from a long time ago that had welled and waited for the coming and the bleak indifference of Ethan.

She shook herself free. She called Mr. Hagan at the grocery store and got a man to come and cut the weeds with a scythe. She paid him five dollars. She asked him if he knew of a dog for sale. He looked off across the field and spat into the grass and did not reply. But the next day he brought her a puppy with short amber hair and long wilted ears like dried autumn leaves. She did not know what kind it was, perhaps a mixture of breeds, possibly a stray, found like Ethan. Its name was Bean.

She hired the black man to make Ethan a swing from a tire in the shed and hang it from the sweet gum outside the kitchen. While she worked she watched Ethan swing by the hour with the puppy beneath him running back and forth, leaping and nipping at the boy's bare feet. His bark was short and mocking. Sometimes she could hear a faint murmur as Ethan bent to the dog. Was he talking to Bean? Or was it the low, chiding music children make for animals? She listened with a kind of hunger in her stillness, till she was dizzy with being in the body of the dog, running back and forth beneath the voice of the child.

Once while he was swinging a bee stung Ethan. She had never heard him cry. She thought at first it was Bean. She ran to the child and searched his body till she found the swelling on the side of his arm. She pulled out the stinger and smeared the wound with baking soda. He held his breath and turned away his head. She spoke to him in soothing tones, telling him not to worry, that the hurt would go away. She held him lightly and touched his hair with her lips. He smelled of earth and leaves and puppy. It was so much like holding Jamie that she grew a little weak. But Ethan stiffened in her arms. She felt his will against her voice and her arms, her lips on his hair. She let him go. How could he be so strong for so long? How could he never need her?

It was as if she held captive a wild sort of bird or some creature of a species she had never seen before. But in a strange way she herself was the captive. She was deeply at his mercy. She took to seeing him in all the corners of the house. Even when she knew that he was swinging in the yard or throwing stones into the pond, she would seem to catch a glimpse of him just beyond her vision when she entered any room. As if he dwelt in all of them, always, forever, and never knew that she was there.

But the child was real enough. A lively glow was in his face when he chased the speckled chickens that had come with the house and nested in the shed. She forbade him to approach the edge of the pond except when she was near. But, standing away from it, he had learned to fish with a pole for the green feathered scum and roll it into balls and toss it at the hens. His legs were always freckled with assaults of insects and scratched with the briars in the underbrush. While he ate his food before her at the table in the kitchen, he smelled of dust and puppy and the tire swing. Even after Bean was gone he smelled of puppy . . .

It was around the first of June that she saw him from the house leaning over something at the side of the road. She knew at once what it was. Without seeing she knew. She hurried to where he knelt to the small crumpled dog. He was touching its nose and its long wilted ears. She was thankful that the car had not mangled or bloodied it. There was only a small wound at the side of the head, but it was quite dead. She dragged it by one foot into the ditch. "Go to the house, Ethan. Bean has been hurt." But he did not stir.

The sun was hot and final. After a time she left him and waited on the porch. She rocked and would not see the buzzards circling in the sky. But her mind grew giddy with their wheeling and troubled with shreds and patches from the day Rachel died. At last she saw a black man passing down the road, and she offered him money to bury the dog in the woods behind the house. While Ethan stood and watched, the old man found a bit of wire, tied Bean to her shovel, and dragged him down her walk. The shovel full of Bean bounced and chimed on the gravel, so light it was. Past the pond and down the field he pulled the shovel behind him in a stately walk. She watched the buzzards follow and Ethan follow.

"Come back," she pled. But the child kept going, running to keep up. She could not bring herself to follow. She stood beside the pond and waited in the sun. She felt old and weak. It was time to make lunch, but she stood with eyes fixed on the small running figure, waiting for the trees to swallow him up. "Watch out for the boy," she called to the man; but he could not have heard, so faint was her voice.

Suddenly before they reached the trees Ethan stopped. Then he turned and started back. She followed his return every step of the way. She searched his face when he neared, but there was nothing to see. No grief or terror or interest or wonder. Just nothing at all. He began to gather sticks and throw them into the pond.

Later he did not seem to remember. It was as if Bean had never been, never come or gone. But she mourned for the dog; she couldn't say why. As if she mourned for herself. She saw in her mind his shallow grave in the woods, his wilted ears filled with moss and crumbling into loam.

She had always taken Ethan with her when she drove the mile down the road to get her groceries at the crossroads store. She left him in the car. It must have been a week after Bean was killed. While she was inside she suddenly heard the sound of voices in the yard. Grant Eris, who pumped gas, was talking to Ethan and Ethan was talking back. Words poured from the boy. She listened in wonder. His voice was strong and high-pitched exactly like Jamie's, the way it was in her dream. She went to the screen door and looked out. They were talking about a fish that Grant had caught and threaded on a branch and now held up to Ethan.

She was deeply stirred. And lurking in the shadow of the airless country store, she grew confused and could not remember the items she had come for. She could not face the boy and surprise him in the act. So she waited inside, faint with the spice-and-honey smell of snuff and the sour-pickle smell and the pungent odor of the spray for flies, pretending to read the labels on the packages and cans. When the voices grew still she summoned the courage to open the screen door where the flies clustered singing and drive away with Ethan through the summer heat.

She thought of telling the boy that she had heard him talking. But she feared the reproach in her words or her voice. So she said nothing to him. But his speaking filled her with a mounting shame. Ethan could talk to others but not to her. It made her glad that she had moved away from town and that her friends were gone, and that she could live alone with the silence between herself and the child.

His silence made her know what she didn't want to know—that the silence of the others had grown with the years. It had come so slowly, year by year, whenever they died or moved away. She could almost pretend that it wasn't there. Like snow it was, which seldom came, but once fell on the town all day, all night, till little by little it filled her world and stifled her steps and the sounds she knew. You can bear the hush if it's slow . . . if it's slow. But then Ethan came, driving his silence like a wedge through hers, making her hear how still it was, making her lose her way in the snow.

Gradually she spoke less and less to Ethan. For she dreaded the stillness that followed her words. And the feel of being wasted and withered away. She could not forget the sound of his voice when he talked to Grant Eris. She heard it in her sleep. Once in her dream he touched her eyes, her lips, her hair. But she could not be sure if it was Ethan or Jamie . . . She woke to her weeping.

Now she talked to herself when she worked about the house. She talked about the years when her husband was alive. One year most of all when they were alone and they brimmed with the shadow and sweetness of life, when he would walk through the door with the gladness in his eyes that was hurtful to see, so fragile it was. And dear little Rachel, pretending to be blind with her eyes crushed tight, groping in the dark to find your face and laugh. She talked about nursing one child or another, the grace of its delicate hand on her breast, the shape and the silk of its golden head. She talked about the past. She was afraid of losing it. She rang up Sam and Ardis but they never answered.

Then she talked to herself about her past with Ethan. She returned in her mind to the day Sam brought him. She longed to go back and begin again. One day, while the boy was playing in the yard, once more she put his clothes away in the drawer. She emptied the old cedar chest of its linens and put his toys inside. She placed the box that had contained them on a shelf of the closet that he could not reach.

The next afternoon she found them again in the box on the floor of his room. His clothes were back in the shabby suitcase. For the first time she noticed the label on the side of the box. It read: T. Sherman, Atlanta, Ga. She examined the suitcase then. In the upper right corner inside the lid was penciled the name of Mrs. Harold Gant and then a Spartanburg address. It came to her suddenly with the force of revelation that Cissie had farmed him out with others—who knew how many?—before he came to Sam and Ardis. Like a seed the fact had lain here all along. And now it was pushing through the crust of her heart. She remembered the inked initials R. M. in the tail of his

T-shirts. She searched for one and found it, with its faint smell of puppy in spite of all her washing. She stroked the canvas-covered suitcase. It was sticky with soil. She lifted his clothes mechanically and folded them again and put them back inside.

Crouched on the floor, her stiff old joints beginning to pain her, she stared at the room with the eyes of the child. Never would he call a room his own. Or a dog his own. Or a person his own. It was this that made her think that in four years of life he'd learned a terrible thing. Something that had taken her a lifetime to learn. Fourscore years, scarcely less, and she was still learning: You give yourself to others and they take your bits and pieces and you disappear.

She was staring down into the clothes she still pressed with her hand. Each garment was separate and alive with his will. His will against her and against this room. She shut the lid upon it. He would never be like her — dependent on another to tell him who he was. Or a house to tell him. He would be himself from the day that he entered her presence, not knowing her or needing her or needing her room or her drawer or her chest. Ethan was contained in his own small body and in the shabby suitcase that had been another's and in the box for his toys that had been another's too.

She got up with effort. The pain in her legs would go away in a while. She stood looking down at his toys in the box. The bear with one eye was head-down among the rest. A child who couldn't feel, one who couldn't belong? No, he wasn't like the child of the niece of Mrs. Ellis. He had tried to belong and had given up belonging. When they moved him yet again, he was packed and ready. The soldiers in his box were still wired to the card. If the chimney crumbled he'd survive untouched. There would be no separations to tear a heart he'd never given. She could envy him for that.

And yet she mourned for him. Beside his bed she sat in the chair, where she had once held Jamie, and rocked and mourned, slipping her hand along the blue cotton quilt, mourning for her own lost self and for him. The sparrows were quarreling in the eaves outside. She could smell the four-o'clocks in the bed below. The sun was slanting through the airless room. It lay along the floor and across her knees. She held it in her lap and watched her rocker slice it into wedges of light . . . shadow and light.

She was afraid of what he knew. He was older than she. It was why she went on rocking the sun in her lap, knowing he was out in the yard beyond, swinging beneath the tree as she was rocking in the room he'd never taken from her. She could hear the iron chain rubbing against the branch of the sweet gum tree. She rubbed her face and arms. She measured her motion to the rhythm of his swinging, willing herself to be enough . . . enough.

At length she got up and went to where he was, but leaving a part of her rocking in the chair. She placed herself before him. Slowly he stopped swinging. But he did not look up. He sat suspended in the tire between heaven and earth. She made the part of her that rocked in his room come to join her in the yard. And she felt that she was swaying before him even now.

She couldn't talk of love. She wasn't sure that she loved him or would ever do so. Or that he understood what love was.

"I am your own grandmother. Look at me," she implored. "Ethan. Please." Her hair had come undone from the motion of the chair. She felt it about her neck and the side of her face. He was looking at the ground. It seemed to her that all the ones she had loved, all her own children, were shrunk into the figure in the circle of the swing and now could deny that she had ever been. But all she really knew was that his will was more than hers.

She knelt to him then, her knees bruised by the bare packed surface of the earth, her hands gripping the tire. "Ethan. Ethan. I have no one left but you." She could smell the faint odor of the puppy still alive in the dust. "I used to have Sam, but he married Ardis and moved away from me and hardly ever comes back. He has Todd and Steve and Gloria, but I hardly ever see them." She stopped for a while. "I have another boy named Jamie who lives in California, but he has a sick wife. She lives in a wheelchair, and so he never comes back. Not ever, Ethan. I had a little girl named Rachel and she grew up and had your mother. But she died, Ethan. Like Bean, you know. So she never comes back. And I had a husband, Ethan, the way Ardis has Sam. But he died too." After a time she said, "And so he never comes back."

She held the swing tightly to keep from falling. "There is nobody in the whole world I can have but you . . . You don't even have yourself unless you have somebody else . . . They gave you to me, and they gave me to you. I belong to you, Ethan. And you belong to me. And I will never give you back. If Sam and Ardis came and tried to take you I wouldn't let them. I would lock all the doors. And if they broke them down I would hide you. And if they found you I would take your hand and run with you across the field and through the trees and over that hill. And if they caught us I would fight them. I would fight my own son. I'm old but I am stronger than anybody knows." Her legs were numb. She felt that she was sinking through the ground before him. "If your own mother came I would fight her too. I would tell her . . . I would tell her you belong to me. Nothing could take you. I would never give you back." Her voice was trembling. Her hands were locked and trembling on the rim of the tire. She could scarcely speak for the violence in her throat and chest. "I will never die and leave you. I promise not to die. And when you grow bigger you can help me not to die." Swaying, she took his face between her hands. "Will you help me not to die?"

She searched his face. He was staring without expression past the trees beyond the hill. The toes of one foot were making scratches in the dust.

She stood up in anguish. Then she walked away. He's a child who can't belong. He can't feel . . . He's a child who can't love. God help me, she said.

God help me because I meant every word that I said. God help me because without him I am losing myself. I'm nothing. I'm lost.

She stumbled toward the pond and walked along beside it. The gnats and waterflies were picking at its surface. She fell kneeling to the face below her in the water. A breeze she could not even feel was stirring it, blurring it into the face in her bedroom mirror without her glasses on.

She closed her eyes, and when she opened them his face was close to hers. His hand was raking the water, shattering their faces into arcs and fragments till they seemed to tumble like her fallen chimney, crumbling into nothing. Like drowning it was. She wanted to turn and leave him, for he was lost too. But she could not move.

And then the water stilled. The shards and slivers mended into faces. They stared at one another down below. Slowly his hand in the water was moving toward her in the depths. It touched her hair. It passed across it, tracing the way it fell in coils against her neck.

She held her breath. She willed herself into the woman in the mirror. And then she could feel his groping hand, seeking in the water her living face.

Her tears fell. Like waterflies they pricked the surface of the pond.

The Quarry

They were always moving, she and Jake and Sam and Luke. They followed the heavy cranes and bulldozers wherever the monsters paused to nose the earth. This time the four of them had settled near a quarry in a rough, abandoned shack. The men were brothers, all with great arms and reddish hair and eyes like gray chinks in a rusty wall. Carrie was married to one of them, to Jake. It almost didn't matter to her which one, they were so alike. Luke had a scar the length of his face where he had fallen from the crane. Sam had lost a finger in one of the machines and mangled another. But unless she was looking at Luke from the left or handing Sam the bread, she could easily mistake the one for the other. Jake, who was the oldest, was heavier than the rest. He had a slope to his shoulders and the freckles on the back of his neck came together. But she noticed that only because they were married.

She cooked and washed the same for all of them. They wore each other's clothes. They treated her the same, hardly seeing her at all but holding her somehow imprisoned in their will. She felt it as a pressure, a crowding together of her senses and her flesh, as if the three of them had jammed her into a corner. It even had the rank and pungent smell of tobacco they liked to chew when they tore into the earth.

When she lay beside Jake at night she could hear across the room the breathing of the others settle into his. On the nights when he would pull her roughly toward him, it was as if they all together held her for a time, and let her go. She was worn out with the weight of them. Then their will for her relaxed and she felt herself adrift in the room as if she'd lost her way. It was strange how they could have her so in thrall and yet not think of her. As if they had dredged her up from some pond or quarry they were digging long ago and then had forgotten her.

If there was money for it they liked to drink beer after supper. They took the radio to the porch and listened to country music for a while. Then they raised their voices, banging words together above the words of the songs. Their laughter had the sound of stones breaking loose and thumping down a hill.

She had learned the trick of standing aside from their laughter, of living prisoned in their realm and hardly knowing it. But it wrapped her up somehow away from the world. Now and then when she was baking bread, the oven smell would free her a little and she could settle in the window with her chin between her knees, her bare feet cautious of the splinters in the wood, and feel all the pressure of the clouds and the crows, the pressure of the leaves and the towhees in the tangle of the jimson weed and the shells of tiny eggs that were caught in the web that billowed from the sill. It was all of it a mothering hand on her skin. It went away when she thought of the men.

The ruined house they lived in was so near the quarry that from the yard a few feet from the kitchen she could see the jagged edge of it. When they left off grinding, roaring, blasting for the day, rocking her fragile cage with senseless thunder, and she had finished with the food and cleaning, the men unbridled her a little and left her to settle in the amber quarry dust that covered all the house. There was a captive softness in her. She was like a talking bird repeating in her mind the words they gave her: "Hell, no . . . " "You got any notion what kinda trouble that is?" . . . "Godamighty, man . . . " She heard their words so much their roughness wore away. There were never any words that were her own.

One day after supper she walked past them on the porch and sat on the slowly rotting steps outside. The house was far gone, with decaying, splintered boards. The floor of it sagged. They must be out of it by winter. The wind would take it over. Once they had eaten, the men would never see her. Their will for her went slack and she was free to sit till bedtime, shelling peas for tomorrow or drawing in the dust with the toe of her sandal, listening to the katydids or listening to the music, with now and then a hoot owl breaking through like a far-off string of a guitar. She could hear them talking up above her with their chairs rocked back, feet propped against the flimsy pillars of the porch. Sam had heard about a convict just escaped from the penitentiary in the county next to theirs. They tried to find the news of it on the radio. "Hell, it ain't no more'n twenty miles away . . . " "Well, if it was me I'd take off into Walker. You know one a them wells we dug up around Jasper . . . " "Hell, Sam they find you in half a day." "Naw, naw, I'd get in one a them dry wells we covered up and I'd hide out in one a them wells. Hell, they covered up with vines . . . " "Hell, Sam, them dogs can find a well. Them dogs has got a smell a you. Hell, Sam thinks all he got to do is take his socks off . . . "

With the laughter their will for her relaxed a little more, like a rope eased out and dropped along the ground. She left the steps and picked her way slowly toward the quarry. She had never been there before, only walked a little from the house while the bread was baking and looked down upon it where it lay half under her, obscured by the scrub oaks, the rocks, and the willows, but here and there a yawning emptiness that frightened her a little. She had turned away from it before.

Now she wanted to get away from the talk of the men. As she walked she found herself surrounded by the breath of pines and the screams of katydids. The path grew so steep that she was almost running, and it seemed to her, as she settled into the motion, that she ran to meet the quarry because it had a will for her. Abruptly she came out on the other side of the wood and the quarry was almost there at the foot of the hill before her.

She picked her way down slowly, clinging to the bitterweed and stripping as she crept the dried and bitter blooms. The small rocks stumbled after her. The pine cones from above bounced before her down the slope, and stones were in her sandals till she pulled them off, and tears were in her eyes from dust that plumed around her. She dragged the hillside with her and her cage world with her, while her life rushed downward to the edge and paused. The flow of all her days was halted at the edge.

Even before she came to it she seemed to see inside that it was empty like herself and had no speech of its own when the man thunder stopped. And like herself it waited to be given words. Breathless at the rim, she saw the giant hollow blood and orange mouth with broken teeth and down inside a band of coral clay, a raw and helpless tongue . . .

She could not see the machines until she leaned far over the ragged willows caught in the corner of the mouth, and there they were beneath her standing docile like cattle in the barn, almost invisible from the red and orange dust that caked their patient bodies.

It was all so quiet. The mouth before her waited speechless. She had no words of her own, but after a time to try its echo she gave it bits of words that had been given her. She heard it swallow them and spit them up.

Then it was quieter than any grave. Till suddenly just below her some rocks were loosened from the wall and went tumbling downward out of hearing. She leaned far over the edge, and through the willows she saw the man on a small, narrow ledge eight or ten feet below. He was lying on his side, body facing the wall, with his head twisted upward. He was dressed in white. She thought at first he was dead. But she looked into his face, which was stubbled with beard, and his eyes that were startled out of sleep. She knew at once it was the convict.

She was not afraid. She looked at him simply with a kind of question. He was still as a rock. She drew back briefly and looked out across the quarry and into the sunset that was striping the sky and into the lonely field beneath and the wood beyond.

Slowly, clinging to a rock for support, she leaned again to see him through the willows below. He had not changed his position. The afternoon light made shadows of leaves on his face and his clothes. Along the sleeve of his shirt was a reddish brown stain that looked to her like blood. She found herself looking straight into his eyes. And they had no will for her. No will at all. They seemed instead to wait upon her will for him. She drew back quickly. Slowly she grew aware of being adrift.

She picked up her sandals and began the heavy climb without looking back. The pine wood was full of night, noisy with frogs and insects. She guided herself by the voices of the men. When she reached the house she put on her sandals and walked straight past them and went to bed . . . All night she slept below the willows on the ledge.

On the following day, as she went about her work, it was she who lay unmoving along the ledge, hidden from the men in her nest of willows. They would come into the quarry from the farther side, where a road had been cut for the truck to maneuver. If she lay stone-still they would hardly see her burning slowly in the sun. But she shrank from knowing what it must be like when the earth around her shuddered with the grinding and the blasting and the red and yellow dust rose to choke her very breath.

In the late afternoon when the men had released her, she took some strips of fresh pork fat she had saved from breakfast and buried them in the fresh corn bread from supper. She wrapped them in a leaf from the sycamore tree and put them in her pocket. She walked past the men sitting dazed with their music. In the weeds near the rusty pump she found the jar she kept there for drinking, and she filled it with water. She pumped a long time to make the water come cold. When the sun was almost down she went again to the quarry, running through the pine wood, sliding down the hill, clutching at the bitterweed, careful of the jar.

She stopped above the ledge. She listened for a time to the great troubled silence that sprang like a gray cat up from the quarry. The shadow below her smelled of rock and ash. When she narrowed her eyes she could see the stubbled earth that swept away to the wood as if it were pastureland, low and grassy, where the cows were grazing in the fields of her childhood. Then she leaned far over, and the convict was there.

He was sitting upright with his back against the wall. She saw his legs in the white pants and his feet in heavy socks and the top of his head with its curling black hair full of red quarry dust and twigs from the willows and a place near the crown where the hair had gone thin. She wound the neck of the jar with a vine she had pulled from a pine in the wood and knotted it and lowered it over the edge, slowly to keep it from banging the rocks, till she felt it caught and jerked like a fishing line. At once she let it go and dropped to her knees, while she clutched at a willow to lean above the ledge.

The stain on his shirt was darker than before and caked with dirt. He held the jar without looking up, as if he had known all along she would come. He drank steadily and deeply. Above him her own throat flooded with cold as if they drank together. Then from her pocket she took the bread and meat wrapped in the sycamore leaf and dropped it beside him. He picked it up quickly and turned from the wall to look into her face. His eyes were red and haunted with the day-long torment of the quarry and his hunger and thirst. She could see how young he was, almost a boy. The cheeks that bloomed from the dark stubbled jaw were flushed with sunburn. Below his temple was a bruise that twisted downward like the scar on Luke's face. Without taking his eyes from her own, he ate what she had brought him in a trance of relief. And when he had finished he frowned at the sky and squeezed his eyes shut. Then she saw that he was looking again into her face, groping at her will for him as on the day before.

She said to him softly, "You hurt real bad?"

He gave no sign. She could taste his weariness like rust on her tongue. She felt herself falling and clung to the willow with both her hands. She lowered her voice. "You better leave here tonight. You hear, now."

He looked at the sky and back to her face. The arms that were bracing her began to tremble and the shudder passed into her shoulders and breast. For a moment she felt herself falling against him, and out of the fear and the rapture of falling she said to him softly, "You kill somebody?" She could see the evening gnats swarming about him and settling like dust on the stain of his shirt.

At once she drew back and fell on the sand and sucked in her breath and rubbed the quivering ache in her arms. The gnats swirled up from the ledge like smoke. When her arms grew quiet she crooned to herself, "You hear, now, you better leave here tonight."

She did not trust herself to look at him again. Her limbs were like water. She stood up slowly and returned to the men.

On the next day she went as before with the food and the water. The convict was gone. The tightness went out of her chest and her throat. She sat on the rim of the quarry and ate with mounting hunger the bread and strips of pork she had wrapped in the leaf. She drank from the glass jar slowly and deeply as the convict had done. And with a kind of happiness she thought of him moving through the wood like a motherless child but growing stronger, moving far away . . .

Then she climbed the hill. The voices of the men growing happy, then quarrelsome, sifted down upon her, but the words were confused. As she neared the words they rounded into shapes that were familiar to her. "Hell, no, Sam . . . " And to her deep amazement they were talking about her. Never in all her life with Jake had she overheard them talking about her. She had to strain to hear above the shrill of the katydids. Sam, it seemed, had found a girl in town. "Hell, Sam, what would we do with another woman?" said Jake. "Two women . . . !" "Well, we gotta think ahead, Jake. Now, how old is Carrie? Well, how old is she, Jake? Hell, ol' Jake don't have the least notion how old Carrie is." She could hear their laughter. The moon had risen behind the wood and was shining all around her.

After they had gone to bed she lay beside Jake. She let the baby she had lost long ago come into her now. She felt it sleeping with the men and waiting to be born. She alone was awake and drifting in her mind over all the room. She got up and by the light of the full moon she looked at herself in the old dresser mirror that was crackled from all their moving around. She rubbed the circles underneath her eyes. She smoothed her hair, still brown with just a little gray. She undid the knot of it and combed it about her neck and over her shoulder the way she used to wear it when Jake would come to call nearly twenty years ago.

At noon when she was serving them the food at the table, leaning over Jake with a bowl of peas, she said to them suddenly: "If you don't know it . . . I'm thirty-eight."

They all stopped chewing and looked at her in mute surprise. Sam and Luke looked at Jake. They went on chewing, their eyes on the food.

At the moment she had said it she felt their will for her relax. But then they chewed her back into it. She went and stood in the doorway. She never ate with the men.

The long quarry summer was turning into autumn. The evenings were cooler and night came soon. Each day at sunset when she crept along the gaping mouth, the quarry and the sky would bay at one another in the same howling color till it hummed in her throat. And she waited till at last they swallowed one another. Sometimes she tossed them a little of the man talk that had followed her through the wood, and something in the sky-earth would swallow up the words. She would sit there mourning in the coolness, hugging her arms, dozing a little, and dreaming the words. Before going home she always looked down upon the ledge where the convict had been.

Her life with the men became a faraway thing. She cooked and cleaned as if the three of them were dreaming all her motions. Sometimes she dropped things flat upon the floor.

Once Jake yelled when she tipped and broke the bowl with the greens. "What's got into you, Carrie? Seems like ever thing you touch you break!"

She stared deep into the rust of his face. "What d'you mean ever thing?"

"I mean what I said."

"You talkin' about the baby?"

"The baby! What baby? There ain't no baby!"

"There was," she said.

"We never had nary baby. Get it outa your head. You cain' call a baby somethin' don't live."

Sam and Luke got up and went to the porch. She could hear them coughing and spitting in the weeds. Jake went after them.

She followed him and stood against the frame of the door. She let the splinters slide through the flesh of her arm. "You tryin' to tell me we didn't have no baby that lived a whole day?"

"Shut up," he said.

She walked to the quarry each day in a dream. Nothing but the quarry belonged to her now. The joe-pye weed was blooming near the edge of the wood. A little farther on, the goldenrod was budding up and down the slope. It was sweeter in the sunlight than anything she knew. But she wanted the goldenrod to leave her alone. None of it was given her to touch in her dream. She began to grow afraid when she thought of the convict.

But once when she was kneeling at the quarry's brink the red and orange valley blew toward her like a flame. A weakness came upon her. She flung herself backward to keep from falling in. Her breath was knocked away and then it filled with sky. In her mouth was a syllable and then another with the green taste of reed along a river's edge. For the first time of all she made a word of her own. She made it out of childhood and the dust in her throat and the rank bitter smell of her hands in the weed. She made it out of nothing, the way the world was made . . .

As soon as she had made it, it fell into the quarry out of hearing, out of mind. She only knew it for a word full of power, and a testing word. A word that could free her to pick up her things and walk away down the road.

Her mind stopped thinking for a while after that. She gathered little rocks and made a circle on the ground. A brown thrasher chirped. He was lost in the weeds. When she raised her eyes, chips of cloud were burning-red and behind them the sky was blooming with the purple of ironweed. Then her mind came back and saw herself walking again down the road. She would walk for a while in her own sweet will and then give it over to the will of the road, to the call of the crows, to the whisper of moss in the forks of the trees. She could see herself walking through low-branching trees as the convict had done.

She covered her face with her bitter-smelling hands. She must make herself strong. Stronger than men. Through the bars of her fingers she saw the quarry below her deeper than hell and broken open and running with blood. It was like herself and had no speech of its own when the man thunder stopped. It lay beneath her helpless as the convict had lain. It looked into her face and seemed to ask her will for it, as the convict had done.

She lay with her face in the sand and the rocks and cried for a little and thought and cried again. Things were born in her mind till the tears at last swept everything away but the quarry helpless and word-less before her, and how it was like her life with Jake and the rest. She must use it for the testing and the proving and the greening of her will. She must make her whole life and the quarry fall down, fall down, whichever one first she didn't care.

Each day she came to it she clung to a willow branch and leaned far over with the testing word. "Fall," she said. "Fall down. Fall down."

It swallowed up the sound of her. She would not stop. She repeated the word till her voice was shriller than the katydids behind her in the wood above.

One day when she spoke a small rock loosened from the wall and plunged downward. It was hardly a thing at all. No larger than a hickory nut. She laid her face against the sand and wept for joy.

She stayed away the next day for fear it wasn't so that her word had moved the rock. After supper Sam went into town and came back with beer. The girl he had brought was out in the pickup. Carrie heard them laugh. "Is Sam aimin' to marry her?" she said to Jake.

"Hell, no," he said. "We got no place to put 'er."

"Is that the onliest reason?"

He cut across her face with his metal-gray eyes. "Hell, you know Sam."

She waited for a while. "Is she purty, Jake? Well, what she like?"

"Cut it out, Carrie."

"Would he be marryin' if I was to leave?"

"If you was to leave and go where?" he said.

In the night she heard the laughter of Sam and the girl. They were on the porch. And then they were quiet. Jake heard their silence and dragged her against him. He smelled of their will for her — stale tobacco, strong and rank. He smelled of the quarry. He poured all the dust of it into her flesh.

Afterwards the rain came down through the roof. And Luke yelled, "HOO!" in the dark. "I'm wet." She heard the bed being dragged and banged. She felt it in her body and drew herself into a hard, tight ball. Through the window she smelled the wet of the sand. A hoot owl called in the sycamore tree. She thought of the quarry gone soft in the rain. The willows were moist and feathered with rain. The stone she had loosened lay cold at the foot of the broken wall.

On the next day she went to the quarry. She filled her mouth with sky and then she called to the earth and the rocks of the earth that circled the pit: "Fall down. Fall down . . ." Her voice was full and gathered to a greatness. She hardly knew it for her own. And this time across from her the great rim tore in a tiny movement of the earth. If she had not been looking directly at the spot she would never have noticed a difference in the land. Suddenly it was there, a little winding crevice no bigger than the stem of a fern in the piney wood behind her, running back into the field, disappearing in the weeds, and down into the crater for the length of her hand.

She sat very still with her heart on fire. It was the way she had felt long ago at the church when they said she was saved and the songs of praise were sung and the arms embraced. But it was far away, almost like another country ago. Each time they moved they seemed to move a little farther from those praising songs. But then she had felt a power in her throat and a singing in her hands . . .

She sat with her eyes upon the crevice till the light was gone.

All the following day she wandered through the red and amber dusty hours. Morning and afternoon the great machines were tearing at the mouth below and shaking her cage. She placed herself inside the smell of baking bread, saving her substance for the work of the evening.

When it was time to go she walked through the piney wood gathering the fern. At the rim she spread the fern down, mounding it neatly to make a place for her to kneel. After she had knelt, she leaned far over, looking down upon the ledge where the convict had been. Intently she thought of him moving far away — in a big city now, walking between the buildings and into the stores and never looking back and no one ever knowing. He was eating something. It seemed to her an apple. She thought of him with gladness.

She tore bits of fern and rolled them in her hands till she smelled of greenness, and she filled her lungs with the green smell of fern. And then she whispered to the ledge to fall. The breath of her whisper was green and free. "Fall . . . fall . . . fall . . . " she chanted slowly, her green voice rising. The ledge beneath her shimmered. A tiny bit of earth broke free of the edge. "Fall . . . fall . . . " The willows shuddered. The ledge began to sway. "Fall . . . fall." It crumbled slowly with a sigh and fell without sound upon the tongue of coral clay.

She lay on the fern and turned her face to the sky. She thought of the very first night with Jake, the night of their marriage when they were all alone . . . before they began to follow the machines . . . and how they lay in bed and didn't sleep all night, how he kissed her throat. Now she could see the moon above the pines. She touched her hair and took out the pin that held it in a knot. She kissed it and combed it with her fingers and braided it over a piece of the fern.

When she reached the house they had gone to bed. She stood in the doorway. It was as if the house had been empty without her, and as soon as she entered it she filled it brimful with the shadows of herself. She was in the moonlight on the bed with Jake. She could feel their will for her a sleeping thing, but she was not adrift as she had been before. Even in the darkness was a path for her feet. She took off her clothes and lay beside Jake and listened to his breathing and the breathing of the others that melted into his. She thought of the baby long ago that had been born too soon and how she heard its breath in the night long after it was taken and buried near the church.

Then she saw herself walking behind the convict in the city. He turned into a street. She was turning with him. When he threw away the apple she picked it up and took out the seeds and held them in her mouth. She thought she would plant them at the quarry's rim.

After that she took to doing something that she could not explain. When she married, her mother had given her some yellow dishes. Most of them were broken with moving from place to place. Only one cup and five saucers were left. Now each morning while the men were tearing at the crater, she took a single saucer and buried it deeply in the trembling earth beside the old well where the ground was soft. It gave her pleasure to dig in the yielding ground, to place in the hole the saucer which she had wrapped in several layers of paper, then replace the earth. She pressed her hands against the little new grave. The grains of sand were live with the movement in the hill. She felt herself alive with the movement in the sand.

The morning she was burying the last one of all, Luke came up from below for water. The sweat was running down the valley of the scar across his face. He stood without a word and looked down upon her. She felt how he called up the will of the others and joined it with his and coiled it around her. She knelt without looking up. She stopped her digging. In her mind she placed her will in the hollow of her hand and then she placed her hand in the hollow of his scar, which was whiter than the rest of him and weaker than the rest. She was almost sorry that she had to do it. He drank a long time from the mouth of the pump, and some of the water splashed onto her hair. Then he washed his arms and his throat and face. But her hand in his scar never washed away. At last he went away from her without a word.

She fell across the little yellow dish she had wrapped in a bit of paper sacking from the crossroads store. Now she knew exactly why she had to bury it and bury the other dishes in the graves nearby. There must be nothing left in the house that was hers from the long-ago time, nothing of her own they could catch in their will. Only the yellow teacup was left in the house. It had a chip on the rim . . . She lay across the dish in the warm, damp ground that moved, even swayed, to the digging below. She fastened her will to the churning machines till it was moving the earth. The earth broke sobbing at her command. She was full of its torment, and full of the child inside her that was crying to be born and would come too soon.

That evening she wrapped the yellow cup in her apron and took it with her to the quarry. It was hard not to drop it as she slid down the hill. When she reached the bottom she sat by the quarry and un-wrapped her cup. She filled it with sand and poured the sand slowly down through the willows where the ledge had been. With her eyes on the wood beyond the stubbled field, she thought of the convict and how she would bring him all the water he could wish. He would drink from the cup, and the child she had lost long ago would be his. "You watch out, now," she would say, "there's a chip on the rim . . ." She stared at the chip and knew without looking that a chip of earth fell from the rim of the crater. She stood up slowly and moved away from the edge. Her will was from the sky and the mountain behind and all the minutes of the years of her life she had waited. She put the cup to her lips and whispered across the rim of it: "Fall . . . fall down."

At once from top to bottom the quarry shuddered. The willows tossed and spun. Pebbles at the rim skittered down and downward into mother-naked earth. Bitterweed was ripped away and tumbled in. The pines above her shrieked. She had a swift glimpse of the coral tongue of clay, how it twisted and rose. The bleeding mouth tore and fell in upon itself.

The red and orange dust hid the face of the sun and the face of the moon that waited in the wood.

When she reached the house she rolled her things into a roundness and wound them and bound them with a string she had saved. And when it was daylight she walked away.

The Christmas Wife

His name was Tanner, a reasonable man in his early sixties, desiring peace, a measure of joy, and reassurance. All that was submerged. The tip of the iceberg was a seasoned smile that discouraged excesses and a way of looking, "That's fine but not today." His marriage had fitted him like a glove, but now his wife Florence was dead for three years. And so it came to pass that Christmas was a problem.

Not a large problem, but one that niggled when the weather turned and got a little worse with blackbirds swarming in the elm trees, on the move. And here he was looking out at the falling leaves, chewing his November turkey in a restaurant down the block, and going nowhere. Except to his son's in California (Christmas with palm trees!), to his daughter-in-law with the fugitive eyes and his grandsons bent on concussions, riding their wagons down the stairs at dawn, whaling the daylights out of their toys. During the long, safe years of his marriage his hand had been firmly, as they say, on the helm. He had been in control. It alarmed him that now he was not in control, even of his holidays, especially of Christmas. A courtly man with a sense of tradition, he liked his Christmases cast in the mold, which is to say he liked them the way they had always been.

Now, the best thing about Thanksgiving was its not being Christmas. It held Christmas at bay. But then the days shortened and the wind swept them into the gutter along with the leaves. And it rained December . . .

He had seen the advertisement several times that fall, a modest thing near the real-estate ads in the Sunday paper, the boxed-in words: "Social Arrangements," and underneath in a smaller type: "Of All Kinds." He had thought it amusing. At the bottom a phone number and then an address.

Actually the address was a little elusive. He passed it twice without seeing the sign. It would have been better perhaps to have phoned, but he wanted to maintain a prudent flexibility. Inside, the lighting was dim and decidedly pink. It proceeded, he saw, from a large hanging lamp that swung from the ceiling, an opulent relic with a porcelain globe painted over with roses. The wind of his entrance had set it in motion and he stood in the rosy bloom of its shadows. He was conscious of pictures in massive frames—one directly before him, a half-draped woman with one raised foot stepping out of something, perhaps a pool—a carpet eroded slightly with wear, a faint sweetish smell of baking food. To his left a man was bent over a desk. Incredibly he seemed to be mending his shoe. Filing cabinets flanked him on either side. For a silent moment they studied each other. What Tanner observed was a dark, smallish face of uncertain age, possibly foreign, with a dusting of beard, a receding hairline, and rimless glasses with one frosted lens. He managed some irony: "Are you the social arranger?"

"I am at your service." The man swept the shoe neatly into his lap, and then he repeated, "I am at your service."

"Yes," Tanner said. "Your ad is tantalizing but a little unclear. The scope of your service . . . "

The man interrupted. "It is very clear. We make social arrangements of all kinds."

"Splendid! Then perhaps I can rely on you."

"We are discreet."

"Oh, I assure you, no call for discretion." Then he laid it before them both, making it seem a spontaneous thing, almost as if the occasion inspired it. The arranger clearly was not deceived. With his unfrosted lens he seemed to perceive how long it had lain on the floor of the mind, how a little each day it had taken its shape and resisted being swept with the leaves to the gutter.

"I am by nature a sociable man." The arranger inclined his head with enthusiasm. "I live alone. My wife is dead. Christmas has become . . . What I require is a Christmas companion. A lady of my age or a little younger. Not handsome or charming. But simply . . . agreeable. Reasonable health. A good digestion, since I shall look forward to cooking for the occasion."

The other was making notes on the back of an envelope. "My secretary," he said, "is out with the flu. An inconvenience." Then he looked up and past Tanner's head. "Overnight, I presume?"

Tanner said lightly, "I've consulted the calendar. Christmas arrives this year on a Saturday. Actually I should prefer the lady for the weekend. But I wish it to be most clearly understood: the bedrooms are separate."

The arranger put down his pencil and adjusted the frosted, then the unfrosted lens. He propelled his chair backward ever so slightly into the burning heart of his files.

"There is a difficulty?" Tanner asked, concealing his unease. "Christmas, I'm sure, is a difficult time. But there must be a few in your files who live alone and would welcome a pleasant holiday with no strings attached." He stared with some irony at the array of cabinets.

"My secretary at the moment . . . Your request is reasonable. We shall consult our files. There is the matter of the fee."

Tanner was ready. "I am prepared to pay a fee of five hundred dollars for a suitable person. And, I may add, a bonus of one hundred to be paid in advance to the lady herself in case she wishes to make some holiday preparation." He had made an impression. He saw it at once. And then, without really intending it, he explained, "I arrive at these figures by checking the cost of a trip to my son's and concluding that this would serve almost as well and be on the whole a great deal more convenient." He turned to go. "In the meantime I shall check on your agency."

"Of course. It is welcomed. Your name and number? A few facts for the files."

"I shall drop by again."

"But your telephone number?"

"I shall be in touch." He left at once. He was again in control of his life, his seasons. The knowledge exhilarated him. He took a deep breath of the chilly air. Halfway down the block he stopped before a store window and studied the objects on display with care. Some plumbing equipment, secondhand it seemed. He was not after all in the best part of town. The bowl of a lavatory brimmed with live holly. In the mirror above it his own face was smiling.

As he moved away he played with the idea of stopping it there, of letting the plan of it be the whole. He sniffed at the edges. The scent of it, crisp, indefinable, a little exotic, was in the wind as he turned the corner.

Before a profitable sale of his business had left him retired and now, as he told himself, dangerously free, he had been an architect. A few years ago he had built for a friend a small vacation house back in the mountains, a comfortable distance away from the city. It was quite the nicest thing of its kind he had done. "Do me something you'd like for yourself." With such an order how could he resist giving all of its contours his gravest attention? He recalled it now with a growing pleasure, how it made its alliance with rock and sky. It was in the year after Florence died, and perhaps it was some of his lost communion that he poured without knowing it into the house.

When he returned to the tiny apartment, haunted with furniture, where he had lived since the death of his wife, he looked at it with a critical eye and found it hostile to holiday cheer. He rang up his friend, who was now in Chicago. What about the house? Using it for the holiday? Well, would you mind . . . ? Well, of course he wouldn't mind.

When the key arrived in the mail he put it into his pocket and went for a walk. He watched the gray squirrels loitering in the park and the leaves crusting the benches and the sun going down through a network of fog. He reminded himself that what he wanted was the mountain air like a ripening plum and the smell of burning wood in the morning. He wanted the cooking. He wanted the house he had made and loved and the presence of a woman, simply her presence, to give it the seal of a Christmas past. There was no woman of his acquaintance whom he could ask to cancel her plans and give him a Christmas out of her life. In return for what? With a woman he knew, there would be the question, the expectation, the

where-are-we-going? to spoil the fine bouquet of the season. In the morning he drove to the arranger.

Actually he had meant to check on the agency, but then it had come to seem that part of the adventure, perhaps the whole of the adventure, was not to do so. So that now the unlikely aspect of the office, with its lamp and the rocking circles of light and its unpleasant piney odor of cleanser, and of the arranger, today without tie and faintly disheveled, did not disturb but even elated him. He was startled and then amused to observe that one of the pictures on the wall had been changed. The one he had particularly noted before of the woman emerging half-draped from a pool had now been replaced by a pasture with cows.

"It occurs to me," said Tanner, "that I don't know your name."

"I have a card somewhere." The arranger rummaged, overturning a vase full of pencils. He was looking flushed, even feverish, but perhaps it was only the rosy light. "My secretary is out . . . " He abandoned the search. "But your name . . . we don't have it. Do we have your name? We require references for the protection of all."

"You have found someone for me?"

The arranger fixed him with the unfrosted eye and gave his desk chair a provocative swivel and coughed for a while. "I believe," he said, "we have just the party." After a pause he propelled himself backward into his files. He caressed the drawers lightly with delicate fingers and opened one with an air of cunning. And swiftly removing a card, he called out: "I think, I do think, this is what you require. I shall read you details, and then of course you can judge for yourself."

Tanner said firmly, "I don't at all wish to know the details. I rely on your judgment." It seemed to him suddenly to spoil the occasion to have the woman read out like a bill of fare.

The arranger was visibly disappointed, as if he had suffered a rejection of sorts. But presently he shrugged and closed the drawer carefully. Still holding the card, he propelled himself forward and into his desk.

Tanner said, "I have here a list of my own: pertinent facts, a reference or two."

The arranger took it and scanned it slowly. Then very quickly the matter was concluded. Tanner was handed a map of the city marked with an X where he was to wait for the lady in question to step from the 2:20 bus on the afternoon of the day before Christmas.

"But I should be happy . . . "

"She wishes it so," said the arranger reverently. And as Tanner was leaving, he called out gravely, "She is one who has recently entered my files. A rare acquisition."

Tanner bowed. "I shall treat her accordingly."

It had occurred to him of course—how could it not have?—that the whole thing could well be a jolly rip-off. While he waited with his car packed with holiday treats, no woman at all would emerge from that bus or the next or the next. The phone would ring on in an empty office. I'm sorry, the number is no longer in use. But because he so richly deserved this Christmas he could not believe it would really be so. And if it were . . . then he would drive slowly and quietly home and slowly and quietly get Christmas drunk. Part of the reward of growing older was precisely this trick one seemed to acquire of holding two possible futures in mind, of preferring one while allowing the other.

He found, on the whole, in the days that followed that it was best to assume that the lady would appear and to give his attention to preparation: a miniature tree, a wreath for the mantel, the mincemeat pies on which he prided himself, the small turkey stuffed with his own invention, the imported Chablis. He had always done most of the holiday meal when Florence was alive. He spent a great deal of time on the gifts, one nice one for her and several smaller things (he wished now that he had permitted himself a few details such as height and weight), a gift for himself in case she failed him in that department.

And of course the day came and the hour struck. With the trunk of his car neatly loaded, he was waiting by the curb. When he saw the bus coming he got out of the car. And there she was, the last to descend, as if she had lingered to look him over. Clutching a small bag, she stood alone looking down at the pavement and then up at him, the winter sun in her narrowed eyes. And she was so unmistakably what she was, a bit of merchandise sent out on approval, that he knew her at once with a catch in his throat and a small despair.

"I'm John Tanner," he offered and gave her his arm, and then as he assisted her into the car, "I've been looking forward to this for days." She wanly smiled.

After that as he drove and kept up a patter of talk to put them both at ease, he remembered how she looked, without looking at her: sand-colored hair (he guessed it was dyed), colorless eyes, a small thin face. He thought she could be in her middle fifties. She rarely spoke, and when she did her voice had a breathless hesitation — very soft, so low that he scarcely heard her.

So he said to her: "Don't be uneasy. I'm really a very comfortable person. This is new to me too. But I said to myself, why not, why not."

She coughed a little.

Then they were climbing into the mountains and the air became damp with fallen leaves and notably colder. When they reached the road that led to the house already the dark was lapping at the trees in the valley below. And around the curve was the house before him exactly as he had made it to be — clean-lined, beached on the rock with pines leaning into it, breasting the wave of sweet gums and oaks that foamed at its base.

He thought how much he had always liked it. "I built it," he said to her. "Not with my hands. Perhaps you were told I'm an architect by trade." He wondered suddenly what she had been told and if it had made her decide to come, or if after all the money was the whole of it.

"I'll go first," he said. "The steps are narrow." With a shyness he had not expected to feel, he climbed through a thicket of wild young shrubs that had marched through the summer to take the stairs. Her plaintive cough like the cry of a bird pursued him into the dusk that gathered about the door. It summoned the longing out of his soul. At that moment he wished that this Christmas were past, over and done with along with the rest. His hands were trembling when he turned the key.

Inside it was dark, with a faint little warmth from the windows that lately had drunk up the sun. He switched on the light and paused to see the great curving room spring to greet and enfold him, exactly as he had created it to do, all the sweeping half-circle of wood and stone, brown, rose, and gray. It calmed and restored him as it always had. He noted the lovely stone curve of the mantel and below it the faggots laid ready to light. Beneath his match they sprang into bloom. And when he turned round the fireshine was kindling the great tile stove, the hub of the wheel, the heart of the house, with its own special curve like a hive of bees. How he loved that stove! He had found it in an old hunting lodge near Vienna where he went for a week after Florence had died. He had bought it and had it dismantled with care and shipped to this place, then reassembled, while he ordered and implored, agonized and exulted, till again every tile was exactly in place—only one of them cracked and that still mourned and unspoken like a guilty secret.

He turned to share it all with the woman behind him, but she was warming her hands in the blaze of the fire. So now he would fill the hive with good oak and a little pine for the seethe and flair. Till the translucent bricks that encircled its base would be gemmed and ringed into amber and garnet. The hunting scenes on the creamy tiles would shimmer and glow and appear to change from moment to moment—the deer and the boar, the flowers, the trees, all richly orange and yellow and brown, as if honey had seeped through the hive to stain them. And the circle of the house would draw close and warm. Guests had always exclaimed: But where, but how? The children accepted without a word. They ran to embrace it and warm their faces. When something is right the children will know it.

He drew the curtains against the night. Then he showed her her room done neatly in white, and assured her the chill would be gone in an hour. While the daylight held he loaded the stove with wood from the generous pile banked against the rock outside. He unloaded food from the trunk of his car and all the rest. He busied himself and refused to think beyond the task at hand. He could hear her coughing in a stifled way.

While he was checking the fire in the stove he recalled with a start and a sense of shame that he had not asked or been told her name. Again she was warming her hands by the hearth. He stood behind her with an armful of wood. "What shall I call you? You must tell me your name." He made it sound as gracious and easy as possible.

She turned to him then. "My name is Cherry."

He found it a fatuous, unlikely name for the woman before him. He wondered if it had been invented for him. He would not trust himself to repeat it. He said instead, "Please call me John."

Her eyes were colorless, he observed again, and reflected the fire, the room, himself. He could find in them nothing of the woman behind them. They seemed in a strange way not to see him. The flesh beneath them looked faintly bruised. The cheekbones were firm and slightly rouged. There were small, parenthetical lines at the corners of a thin and somber mouth, which he noted with relief was free of rouge. He said to her kindly, "You seem to be coughing. Perhaps we have something here that would help."

She withdrew from him then. Her eyes shut him out. "Oh, no, I'm fine. It's just . . . well, I had the flu but I'm over it now. But when night comes on . . . I cough just a little."

He reassured her. "The flu is everywhere. I've really remarkable resistance to it."

"I'm really quite well."

"Of course," he said and winced to recall that clearly he had specified reasonable health. He could explain now her stifled voice in the car. "I've made a little light chowder for supper. Something very light. It will warm you up and be just the thing. I've always made it for Christmas Eve."

"That would be nice. I can help you with it."

But he would not have it. He placed her in a chair before the fire with a throw from the sofa around her shoulders and told her to rest her voice and be still. Then to get her into the spirit of things he found the wreath made of ribbon and holly and balanced it on the mantel before her. And he added a length of pine to the stove. He opened the vents to make it hum for her like a hiveful of bees in the manner its maker had meant it to do—a trick of construction he had never fathomed. The tiles had taken on a splendid sheen. He wanted to tell her to turn and watch.

While he was warming their supper in the kitchen, she came and stood in the archway, her eyes pale as glass, her hands, transparent with blue veins, clutching the sill like roots. He had put on his dark-rimmed glasses for the work. She looked at him with a kind of alarm as if he became even more the stranger, almost as if she surprised an intruder. But he led her back to the chair by the fire. He scolded her heartily, "I want you well by Christmas." The words and the gestures sprang naturally out of the last years with Florence.

He served them both from trays by the fire, making it all seem easy and festive. She ate very little. He poured her a glass of Tokay, and while she sipped it, her face now pink from the fire, he got out the tree and began to trim it with the tiny carved figures he and Florence had found in a shop in Munich before their son was born. He told her about them. She put down her glass and began to help. One of the small figures slipped from her fingers. When he bent to retrieve it he saw that her eyes were swimming in tears. "Don't worry," he said. "They're quite indestructible."

She fought for control. "It's my glasses," she said. "I don't see without them."

"Of course. Where are they? I'll get them for you." He rose at once.

She drew in her breath. "I forgot to bring them."

Or had she thought he would find them unpleasing? He was really impatient. Should he have specified in the beginning that he wanted a woman who could manage to see?

Finally he asked, "Shall I put on some music? Or would you just rather call it a day?" He did not like to say "go to bed," an innocent phrase that had been corrupted.

"It's what you want."

"It's what you want too."

But she shook her head. She was paid to pleasure him, to enjoy what he offered. He was suddenly struck with how easily the shape of a thing could change and take on the color of prostitution. A practiced woman would take care to conceal it, but in her innocence she underlined it. He rose and removed the throw he had placed on her shoulders. His voice was grave. "If I'm to have my way . . . I want you to have a good night's sleep."

The evening was gone. He could not retrieve it, nor would he have done so. His heart was heavy. He lowered the lights. Her face was uncertain but she moved away past the stove that sang softly like a bird in the dusk, throwing its shadows on floor and wall. She looked at it briefly and passed without comment. Perhaps she could scarcely see it at all. Her gesture summed up for him the failure of the day.

He tried to sleep. The wind had risen. The pines above his bedroom were stroking the roof. In the room beyond he could hear her coughing. Wasn't she after all what he had ordered — a nothing who would not intrude or assert or assess or be?

He tossed in despair. Christmas is dangerous, it's too hot to handle, it's a handful of roots breeding — what did the poem say? — memory and desire. Get another day. Fourth of July, Labor Day. Don't pit yourself against Christmas. You lose. You can't contain it. It runs backward into a shop in Munich. It echoes . . . It's calling your own name down a well.

He slept a little. And in his dream the social arranger took off his glasses and lo, behind them his eyes were laughing. The eye once hidden by the frosted lens was crinkled with laughter. Why are you laughing? Tanner approached him and saw, peering, that the eye was a stone and cracked into pieces.

He awoke, dispossessed. The dark ran liquid through his veins. The wind whipped him into some distant gutter.

When daylight came he lay grimly rehearsing his script for the day. If order prevails all things are possible and even tolerable. The key of course is to be in control. His shoulder was stiff from hauling the wood. He had raised his window to sleep in the cold, and now he heard the sound of a distant axe breaking, breaking the early day.

He had the turkey in the oven, the pilaff thawing, and the salad prepared before she appeared for her morning coffee. The patches of dark were still under her eyes, but her face was rested. She seemed to have taken great care with her dress. Her sand-colored hair was combed back from her face, and now he decided the color was hers. He could see the gray. She was wearing a wine-colored jumper with a gray-green, high-necked blouse beneath. They might be a nod at the Christmas colors. There was something childlike about her dress and her slender figure, and touching about her desire to please.

He drank a third cup of coffee with her, and some of the grayness drained out of his soul. She pronounced the smell of his cooking agreeable. In the glance of her eyes around the room there was something of readiness, almost he might say of anticipation. And suddenly the day began to be possible.

"Were you warm enough in the night?" he asked.

"Oh, yes. Oh, yes."

"You're not coughing today."

"Oh, no. I'm well."

After he had coaxed the stove into shimmer and the comfortable song it could sing in the morning after a night of lying fallow, he drew the curtains away from the windows, a tender curve of them like a sickle moon, the way he had planned them in the beginning. The mist was milk in the pines and the hollows.

Before she arose he had laid his gifts for her around the tree. She looked at them with a troubled face. "I didn't know."

"How could you know? It would spoil the surprise."

But she left him quickly and returned with an unwrapped heavy tin. "I was saving it for dinner." She handed it to him, then took it away and put it with the other things beside the tree. His heart misgave him. It was fruitcake of course. He had never liked it. But what else came in round tins painted with holly and weighed enough to crush the bones of your foot?

He put on some music. He made her sit in state on the sofa. Then he found his glasses on the sink in the kitchen and put them on her. "I want you to see. Can you see?" he asked.

She looked around her and down at her hands. "Oh, yes, I can."

"Are you sure you can?"

"Oh, yes. Oh, yes."

"Well, at least you will see things the way I do." He had to laugh. She looked like a small, obedient child who was given permission to try her father's glasses. They diminished her face and gave her an owlish air of wisdom. Then he handed her the packages one by one — first, the teakwood tray, then a fragile porcelain cup and saucer with a Christmas scene. For Christmases to come. And to remind her, he said, of this very day. Then a small, lacquered music box that played a carol. While it finished its song he opened the tie he had bought for himself and exclaimed at the colors. He declared that a friend had secretly left it on the seat of his car. She held her things on the tray in her lap and watched him with pale and troubled eyes, their trouble magnified by his glasses. "Do you like them?" he asked. "Oh, yes. They're lovely." Then he watched while she opened the tall ribboned box with the figurine, a bit of Lladro that came from Spain. She drew out the blue-and-gray girl with the pure, grave face and the goose in her arms. She held it silently. Then she touched the smooth, child's head with her hand. "Do you like it?" he asked.

"Oh, yes. I do."

"I knew you would like it." She looked at him, puzzled. "Oh, yes, I knew it . . . It reminds me," he said, "a little of you."

What he meant, he realized, was that Florence would like it . . . and that it also reminded him a little of her. But there was one box more, the largest of all. "But you've given too much." She was reluctant to open it, almost distracted. He could tell she was thinking of the whole of her cost, the somber transaction with the seedy purveyor.

"What is too much? This Christmas has never happened before." And he added gaily, "Whatever you don't like will have been too much. We can toss it into the stove and burn it."

She smiled at that and opened the box. She lifted the dark green, floor-length woolen robe, severe, elegant, very formal. "Try it on," he commanded. She did so obediently. He crossed the room to appraise it from a distance and pronounced it too long. He saw with dismay he had bought it for Florence, her height, her coloring. But it seemed to do now surprisingly well. It coaxed her colorless eyes into green. "I like it on you. You must leave it on till the room is warm."

But she took it off at once. "It's much too fine." She folded it carefully and put it back in its box.

The dinner went well, and she seemed to enjoy it. He insisted she wear his glasses while eating. It was prudent, he said, to consume nothing on faith. At his urging she took a second helping of pie. He allowed himself a generous slice of her cake and declared it superior. He toasted her fruitcake, herself, and the day. Her face was flushed to a pink with the wine. Her hair fell softly against her cheek. She brushed it away with the back of her hand, which was worn and expressive, with a tracery of veins. He had seen such a hand on a painting in Prague.

He allowed her to rest for a while after eating. Then he told her about the lake below the house, hidden from view because of the trees. "Would you like to walk down?"

"Oh, yes," she said.

At his bidding she put on a sweater he had packed for himself and then her coat. She drew a flimsy scarf over her head. He looked with doubt at her fragile shoes. But she said they were all she had brought along. "No matter," he said. "I'll keep you from falling."

Outside it was sunless and clear and cold. The mist had vanished. The path was hardly a path at all. He had to steady her over the rocks. She was light and insubstantial against him. In the trees around them festive with moss the squirrels were stammering, cracking their nuts and spitting the shells. Under their feet the acorns of water oaks crackled like flames. And then the lake was down below like a rent in the fabric of moss and leaves. Strange birds were skimming it looking for fish, with haunting cries that poured through the trees and summoned them to the water's edge.

He guided her down. Once she slipped but he caught her and held her safe. She was shivering a little. "Are you cold?"

"Oh, no."

He held her arm tightly to reassure her. The lake was polished and gray as steel. Across it a line of young bamboo was green, as if it were spring on the other side.

"It's very deep. And somewhere in the middle is a splendid boat that sank beneath me without any warning."

He watched her eyes look up and smile. "Were you fishing?" she asked.

"Yes, that I was. And the fish I had caught went down with the boat. When I came up for air they were swimming around me laughing like crazy."

He had made her laugh, in the way he could always make Florence laugh when he sounded foolish. Her laughter warmed him in some deep place that had long been sunless. Not the laughter itself, but the way he could pluck it out of her throat, summon it out of whatever she was.

He ventured, regretting the small deception: "You remind me of someone I used to know whose name was Beth. Do you think you would mind if I called you that?"

"Oh, no."

He was more than relieved to be rid of the name which he could not bring himself to repeat. He was holding her firmly. The edge of her scarf fell against his face as if she had touched him. It released him into the cold, still air. The birds were circling, ringing them with their plangent calls, weaving them into the water and trees. She coughed a little and the shudder of her body against his own was mirrored down in the polished lake. Her image in water joined to his was clearer to him than the woman he held.

As if it had lain in wait for him there, he remembered a time before the boat had vanished. It was in the summer they were building the house, the only one then for miles around. The workmen had all gone home for the day. He rowed himself to the middle of the lake and waited. He never knew why it was he had waited. And suddenly along the line of the shore a woman was walking who seemed to be Florence: the shape of her body, the way she moved, as she was in the years before her illness. Her head was bent. She was looking for something at the water's edge. He could see her reflection just below moving with her like a walking companion. Abruptly she knelt and, leaning over the slight embankment, she plunged one arm deep into the water. In the waning light he could see the gleam of her bare white arm as it disappeared. For a terrible moment he was sure she would fall and join the woman in the water below. The whole of the lake was moving in ripples, around him, past him to where she knelt. He could not call. He simply willed her, willed her to rise. And she rose and looked at him across the water. And then she turned and walked into the trees. He had never known who the woman was . . . or if she was.

The woman beside him coughed. "Do you swim?" he asked.

"Oh, no," she said.

He waited a little. "Would you like to go back?"

"Whatever you say."

They climbed the hill slowly, clinging together, pausing at intervals to catch their breath and release it in mingling clouds to the air.

A rising wind sprayed their faces with leaves. He felt they were plunging deep into winter. The rock supporting the house above them loomed pearl gray in the evening light. Below them the lake had been sucked into shadow.

In the night he awoke with a cold, clear sense that Florence had called him. He lay still listening. But of course not Florence. Then he heard the sharp cough, but it did not come from the room next to his. It came from another part of his world, and it seemed on the move like the call of a bird, caged in the circle he had made of a house. It shattered his dark. Finally he put on a robe and found her in the living room with her hands and her body pressed to the stove. She stood in darkness. But she had pulled the drapery back from the window, and in the moonlight he could see her clearly, motionless as if she were carved in marble.

He switched on a lamp. She turned to him quickly a face that was stricken with grief and shame. "I'm sorry, I'm sorry."

"Were you cold?" he asked.

"A little cold. But the cough is worse when I'm lying down. I was afraid of waking you."

He saw that she had thrown over her own dressing gown the robe he had given. "You're not to worry. I'm here to help." He noted her trembling and built up the fire.

"I'm sorry," she repeated. "I've spoiled it all."

"You haven't spoiled a thing." He fetched her a chair.

He found a jar of honey in the kitchen and a lemon he had packed; and he fed her spoonfuls of the mixture as if she were a child . . . as if he were giving Florence her medicine when she woke in the night.

"Thank you," she said. "I'm so sorry."

"You mustn't talk."

She sat by the stove, her body subdued, in an attitude of profound despair. He pulled the robe close about her shoulders and waited silently beside her chair. He felt he was on the edge of something, a depth, a life he did not want to explore. A lonely woman who had waited for years for a door to open and now was in terror of seeing it close? He drew away. Nothing is simple, he said to himself. Nothing is ever, ever simple. Though what he meant by it he could not say. He saw his own life as an endless struggle to make the complex simple.

Commanding her silence, he turned out the lamp. He drew up a chair for himself and sat near her, and waited as he had waited in the night with Florence after the stroke had forbidden her speech. The moonlight was cold on her trembling form. The circle of light at the base of the stove drew him down and ringed him with glimmering warmth. He sat half dozing in a strange sort of peace, because it was good to be with a woman on a Christmas night. And because he had bound her voice and its power to give him more.

After a time, when her trembling had stopped, he gave her another spoonful of syrup and sent her to bed with the rest of it.

In the night through the wall he could hear her weeping. He lay with some reservoir within him filling with tears. The walk through the wood had brought a memory of Florence, the sharpest one. She had been moving ahead through the trees of another wood. He had heard the rustle of her shoes in the leaves, and then nothing. He thought she had stopped to peel moss from the bark of a fallen trunk for her garden at home. And so he had come on her fallen body. Then the long limbo of her stroke and death, when slowly, slowly she had withdrawn. As he thought of it now, and had scarcely let himself think it before, there had been a period before that day when she had withdrawn herself ever so lightly. In fact for some years: "Whatever you think . . . whatever you like . . . if it's what you want." His will was hers, his desires her own. It was almost as if her helpless years were a further step in a long dependence. He had liked the deference of her will to his. He liked to arrange the life for them both. Perhaps it was true — he saw now it was — he had struck her down in her vital self and summoned compliance out of her soul. And in compliance was bred withdrawal. Yet surely, surely it was what he wanted. Making a house or making a marriage, always he had to be in control. Her death had ended his long dominion. He must admit he had reigned with spirit . . . and a certain flair.

Genial husband, genial host. And now in the dark he knew himself as the social arranger. That seedy figure in the heart of his files he had conjured out of his own deep need. The woman weeping behind

the wall — weeping for a reason he could not explain — was made to
his order. He remembered with shame how he had denied her a past
or a name. As if he would grant her permission to be . . . what he
wished, when he wished.

Sometime before dawn he made peace with himself, as a man
must do.

He awoke with a start. The windows were opalescent with ice.
The needles of the pines were threads of crystal. Their boughs lay
heavy along the roof. He rose to shake up the fire in the stove with
a thunderous clamor, for the final time. He built the flame on the
hearth again. And when she emerged, her eyes faintly rimmed, the
lines gone deep at the corners of her mouth, he stood before her in
new humility. Today he allowed her to help him with breakfast, a
good one to last them for the drive into town. Then while the kitch-
en was alive and steaming with the cleaning up, he asked: "If you
hadn't come . . . " He began again. "If you had spent Christmas in
the usual way, where would it be?"

She was washing dishes and did not answer. He heard her silence,
again with relief. He said with good humor, "But the rule is you
have to take half the leftovers back to wherever it is you would be if
you weren't here now." He was restored as the genial host.

After a little he went into the living room and stood at the crescent
line of the windows. He could see the frozen forest below, shimmer-
ing with amber light in the sun. Beside him the warmth of flame on
the hearth. It seemed to him that this was enough forever — the ice-
filled trees, the flame-filled room in the midst of ice, all this ice with a
heart of fire. He was conscious that she had entered the room. For a
moment he asked for the trees along the mountain road to break
beneath their burden of ice and cut them off for another day.

He turned to see her. She was pressing her hands to the tiles of the
stove — worn hands the color of the ancient tiles. "I'll show you a
secret," he said to ease her. "There's a tile that was cracked, and no
one knows where it is but me. And I've never told."

She seemed not to hear. It was almost time to put her back in the
box, like the blue-and-gray girl with the goose in her arms. And so he
told her, "I shall always remember this time . . . these days."

She sucked in her breath and turned away. He stopped and waited. She began to cry. "What is it?" he asked.

But she turned again and walked to the fire. "You're so good," she said in a stifled voice. "You're so kind."

He was moved. "But that shouldn't . . . "

"Oh, yes. Oh, yes."

He said something he had not intended to say then, perhaps never to say: "But it doesn't really have to end with this . . . But I can't go on picking you up at a bus stop."

She faced him, weeping, shaking her head.

"You've not enjoyed it?"

"Oh, yes. Oh, yes. It's the loveliest time I've ever had."

"Then why . . . ? I assumed . . . Why would you be in his files . . . why would you be willing to come at all unless . . . " Then a kind of light seemed to dawn in his mind, as if he had known it all along. "You work for him," he said. "You're the secretary who was out with the flu."

She did not deny it. She wept on into her handkerchief, coughing as if he had called up her illness. "Are you?" he asked. She nodded her head. She could not speak. "But it's all right . . . it's all right. Why should I care? I really don't care if you work for the charlatan. He made this weekend possible, didn't he?"

She gave him a final, stricken look. "I'm his wife too."

"His wife!"

She wept.

He was stunned. "But why?"

Through her tears she told him. "There was no one else. And we needed the money. You don't know. The bills."

"But his files . . . the files."

"They're full of other things, not names: cleaning aids . . . other things. We have nothing at all. I bought these clothes with the money you gave." Her voice sank to a hopeless whisper. "He said I should do it. It would be all right. He said you were safe."

"Safe!"

"He said you were . . . "

"Safe?"

She did not answer.

"No one is safe! How could he send you out like this? How could he know I was safe, walking in out of the street like that?" His anger released him from hurt and chagrin. He paced the length of the curving room. He said to himself: I've been taken . . . had.

He turned to her from the end of the room. The stove beyond him was deep in whispers. The ice outside slipped and fell from the trees. "Can you approve of this . . . man? Can you love this man?"

"He's my husband," she wept.

He was forced to see with what grace she suffered them both.

And so he did indeed put her back in the box. He drove her to the bus stop and waited in the car, talking lightly of the winter ahead and the spring when perhaps he would take a trip to the West. When the bus arrived he helped her on with her packages. The music box gave a stifled cry. He saw her safely seated at the rear. Then he watched while her bus moved off and away, picking up speed with a grinding of gears, moving faster and farther away past the winter and into spring and on through a shower of summer leaves, and never reaching her destination.

The Singing Well

She was Emilu, named for two dead aunts, their names rammed together head-on like trains.

Her house was built in a wooded hollow for a reason that nobody seemed to know. "I feel like I'm smotherin' down in a barrel," her mother would say when the summer heat came. And when it would rain for a month in the winter, "I feel like I'm swimmin' around in a bucket." The house was an island. The full moon floated its face at the door. Jo-Jo said it was like a castle that had a moat. "It would be great if we got attacked." His mother replied, "That thought don't do a thing for me . . . Ray, I'm lookin' for the day I can move to the top of a hill and watch the raindrops pass me by."

To make it worse, her mother said, her father had circled the hollow with corn. "Ray, it's like you took every breath of air there is." Before he plowed it down in the fall, the winds would rattle the cold dry stalks and ribbon leaves. They could hear the clamor with windows shut. "Ray, I can hardly hear myself . . . " "Wow!" said Jo-Jo. "We're bein' attacked! Pow pow pow!" "Jo-Jo, will you stop this pow pow pow." And Emilu said, "This family is nuts."

It was her private and public opinion.

She was past eleven, going on twelve, and out of the torment of school for a while. The days of summer were long at first and then ran away like a rabbit flushed out of a blackberry bush.

It scared her some, not just to be looking down the barrel of school. Eleven years old and going on twelve, she was staring right now both ways at once. She had got her feet planted plumb in the ground to keep from getting any older at all. But all the time she needed to get there. She had to know more. And she thought as she lay on her back in the corn, racing her feet a toe at a time up the head-high stalks, letting one foot, then the other win: How you gonna handle these things that come up? Get around these grown-ups pushin' you into some kinda way you never wanted to be? But if you grew up so you could outsmart 'em, then you did what they wanted. You got yourself grown and no turning back. And maybe you couldn't stand it that way and waited around and hoped you would die, with cancer even, just to get it over. The way it seemed to her a lot of them did.

She knew that she was smarter than Melissa, her sister who grew up enough to get married. And smarter than Jo-Jo, who was off at their Uncle Joe's for the summer. But it wasn't sufficient. This thing coming at her was as big as a barn. Sometimes it was a freight train running her down. Sometimes she felt she was in there swimming and going under for the final time.

And then her grandfather came in July and she grabbed ahold of him to keep afloat.

How can you grow up when you have a grandfather like a Santa Claus with his beard cut off and he calls you little daughter and feeds you peanuts one at a time?

When he got out of the truck with her father, bigger almost than she had remembered, her mother said, "Emilu, run carry that box he's got in his hand. Lord knows what's in it." Emilu ran and dropped it hard coming up the steps. It flew apart, and an old uniform fell into the nandinas. And her mother said, "Well, I might've known. Well, bring it on in."

He was in his room when she got it together. The door was ajar. She waited in the hall. When she heard silence she edged in slowly with the box in her arms. He was sitting on the brass bed all hunched over, his chin down into the front of his shirt. His chest caved in and his face was like he was sorry he came.

She said to him then, "I folded it good." They looked at one another across the years between. Her mother had said he was seventy-seven. "It's got real pretty buttons sewed on."

He must have been, easy, six foot tall and big around. Like a football player with everything on, and shoulders big and round like a bear's. He had a great head of wavy white hair that curled around and under his ears. A sunned kind of face without many lines and blue fire eyes that were almost hidden by the shelf of his brow and the white eyebrows that went so wild they must have been raked in the wrong direction. His hands were huge and brown from the sun, with white hairs matting on the backs of his fingers. His glance wavered, then returned to her. There was something in it different this visit from last.

"Are you Melissa?" he asked.

She was surprised and even shocked at his words. "No, Grandpa, I'm Emmy." He had called her that.

"Emmy?" He looked at the mirror above the green-painted dresser. "Not Melissa?"

"No, sir . . . Melissa got married and lives in Lafayette."

His glance swept her with such a lost look that she told him again, "I'm Emmy, sir."

He was very strange. But his blue eyes beheld her without a rejection. "Emmy . . . Emmy . . . " He moved a little inside his great frame and rubbed his arm. "I'll tell you how it is."

She waited for him to tell her but he seemed to have forgotten or thought better of it. "What, Grandpa?"

His eyes circled the room. "Is this the same room I stayed in before?"

"Sure, Grandpa."

"Same mirror and all?"

"Sure it is . . . You don't remember?"

He looked at her hard. "I'll tell you how it is: I don't recall you."

She was really amazed, but she tried not to show it. "We played euchre and all. You taught me, remember? Slap Jack. Ever day."

He shook his head slowly. "No. No, I don't recall." He spoke so sadly that she wanted to run away. "But it seems like whoever you are . . . it seems like a good thing, you standin' here now." He smiled at her almost. "We was good friends, you say?"

"We played euchre ever day."

"What did I call you?"

"Emmy. You called me Emmy, like everbody does exceptin' Mama."

"You feel right. Somehow. How old would you be?"

"Eleven last month. I was nine before."

She couldn't wait to tell her mother.

"We shouldn't have him this summer. I said so to your father. He looks healthy. I will say that. I can't deny he's a downright specimen of health." Then she flattened her lips. "But his mind . . . "

"What's wrong with it?" said Emilu.

"Well, it's gone, that's all."

Emilu was defensive. "He talks all right."

"Talks!" her mother said and turned away to run water on the beans. "Just stay out of his way."

"Why?"

Her mother flung a sideways look at her. "Folks like that get full of notions." And she left the room with the water still on.

Emilu sucked the knuckle of her finger. Her mother never came right out and answered a question. You thought you had her on the track and then she ducked into a side road.

Emilu ran out the back and circled the house. She could look through his window and see him on the bed. He hadn't moved. He seemed just the way he was two years ago. They stared at each other the way she had looked at a deer she met once that Jo-Jo had trapped and he looked at her knowing she wasn't the one did it but there he was in the fix he was in. She came in the front door and down the hall to him again.

He seemed glad she was there. She sat down at length on the chair by his bed. Then he opened his suitcase and rumpled around and came up with a bag of peanuts. He sat back on the bed and gave one to her and one to himself. They were very still while they looked at one another across their chewing.

That night, before she went off to sleep, she could hear him moving in the room across the hall, then a scraping sound, a sour wail of furniture being dragged across the floor. It went on for some time. She could hear her mother in the room next to hers. "My

God, what's he doin'? I can't stand it, Ray." She heard her father's muffled voice . . .

And then it was daylight. The wind outside was rattling the shutters. She woke up thinking it was still the furniture being dragged around, then knowing it wasn't.

When she went to his room she saw the dresser standing slap across the corner. And now a square of dust marked the place it had been. He was sitting on the bed looking out of the window at the waving trees.

She was full of the morning. "How come you moved the dresser around in the night?"

He looked at her with haunted eyes.

"Grandpa . . . how come?"

He shook his head. "It ain't the same room," he said at last.

She started to tell him that it really was, but she stopped herself. She could hear the geese being chased by the dog. She could hear the bus passing, rounding the curve, and then taking the hill. She sat on the bed and swung her feet. "You wanta play euchre?"

He shook his head. "I don't recall it none."

"You taught me, Grandpa. I could teach you how. I remember it real good."

"Wouldn't serve. I'd fergit."

She said with pride, "I never forgot nothin' I ever knew."

He shook his head in wonder. "It goes," he said. "I can't figger where it goes, but it goes all right . . . I think when it all goes what'll I be then? What'll I be just a settin' somewhere? Sometimes it scares the livin' hell outa me."

She swung her feet. "I know ever dadblasted thing ever happen to me."

"You think so, little daughter. But there is things gittin' away from you in the night when you fergit to hold on."

She shook her head. "Not me. I got it all somewhere. In my head, I reckon."

"'Course you ain't live long. There just ain't that much."

"There's a plenty, I guarantee. There is plenty done happen."

"Well, hold onto it, little daughter."

"I'm a holdin' on."

She got up and walked to the square of dust where the dresser had been. With her toe she scraped a circle and a zigzag line. "Slap Jack is nothin' to it. How long you figger you can hold on to somethin'?"

"No way a tellin'. Hard to say, little daughter."

She swallowed twice. "You called me that before . . . when you were here before. You called me little daughter."

"Did I, now? I musta liked you mighty well."

"Oh, you did. You did. Better than the others. Sometimes we sung songs. On the porch. In the dark. We sung 'Old Black Joe' and 'O Suzanna, don't you cry for me' . . . " She was pleading now.

"I don't recall," he said.

A feeling of hopelessness swept over her. They mourned together.

"We got to start over," he told her gently. "You willin', little daughter?"

She was sad in a way she had never been before. He patted her hair. "You willin', little daughter?"

But she did not reply.

"Was you wearin' your hair a little different?" he said.

"Just the same," she said faintly and shook her brown mane. "Chopped off straight. I just can't stand it no other way."

"You willin', little daughter? It's hard," he acknowledged. "I know it ain't fair."

Her voice was uncertain. "But it seems like you don't want to start over, Grandpa. I could help but it seems like you don't want to try."

He was silent for a while. "I got somethin' on my mind, little daughter, to 'tend to . . . I can't think a nothin' else. It's on me night and day."

"What is it?" she said.

"It's a misty thing now. But what's so strong is how good it was. Good. Good. If I could remember it. If I could git it back once and then tell somebody who wouldn't let go . . . "

He looked at her with something in his eyes like a plea. "That's where maybe you could come in."

"Where, Grandpa?"

"You gonna come in two ways, little mother. You gonna help me remember and then you take it from me and you don't let it go."

"So I can tell you again in case you forget?"

"No . . . no. I wouldn't need it again. Just need you to have it. Just to not let it go. Now, I'm gonna die. Some day not far away. Who cares?"

"I care, Grandpa." Then she said, disbelieving, "But some day I'm gonna die."

"Don't you think it. You gonna live forever. And if you felt yourself slippin' you could tell somebody. You could tell the best person you happen to know . . . like I'm tellin' you . . . when I git it back."

"Am I the best person you know?"

"You are the one best person left with any walkin'-about sense." She swung her feet. "That ain't the general opinion around here."

"It's mine," he said.

"What about Grandma?"

"Best woman I ever knew. But she's gone, you know."

He stared out the window. "There was a thing that happened to me once. Best thing that ever happened. I never told nobody, it was that good."

"You gonna tell me?"

"I'm gonna tell you if I can recall it. *If* I can recall it. If . . . if."

"If it was that good, how come you forgot it?" She was sorry she'd said it, for his face clouded over.

"I ain't entirely done that, little daughter. There's somethin' still there. But it don't come together. I hold on to one thing and somethin' else goes . . . It's gotta be the right kinda weather for holdin'. Today is no good. There's a wind a-blowin'. We could work on it, maybe we could tomorrow."

She listened to the sucking of wind in the eaves and beyond it the murmur of wind in the corn.

"When it blows I can't recollect one damn thing."

He did not seem to want to talk any more. She studied a stain on the papered ceiling and decided it looked like a crow or a buzzard. After a while she got up. His eyes had gone into the cave of his brows. "Grandpa," she said, "you gonna recollect it. I double-dog guarantee it you will."

She went outside and raced up the bank that surrounded the yard. She walked barefoot through the rows of corn. The silk was bronzed and hung from the ears in tassels that seemed to beckon the wind. She pulled some away and stuffed it into her own two ears. She closed her eyes and between the rows wandered deaf and blind, groping for stalks, plunging, weaving one row with another. But still she could hear a bird mournfully chirping. She followed its cry. "I hear you, little bird . . . I'm comin', little bird . . . You need me, little bird." She stepped on a rock and opened her eyes. Standing on one foot, she spit on her toe and rubbed it up and down and sideways.

When she passed his door again it was still open and she looked inside. He was sitting in the chair. The box for the uniform was in his lap. He looked at her as if she had never left the room. "I see a well . . . But it's blowin' too hard. Too hard to tell."

At last she said, "Grandpa? What happened had a well?"

He moved his head slowly from side to side. "Hold on to it," he said.

That night before she slept she seemed to hear him singing in his room across the hall. It was a strange kind of tune. But not a tune at all, as if the notes got lost and he had to start again.

Her mother was a woman who put up food. When she was settled down into it somebody seemed to have started a war, and Emilu said the next bus that came she was climbing on. Each day was closer to the end of the world till it felt like a yell coming out of her chest. You better clear out or you'd get yourself sliced and chopped and crushed and scorched and stirred, boiled over and mopped from the stove and the floor. Her mother pink-faced, with pale hair loose and hanging in strings that had got in the jam or the succotash. "Emilu, will you hand me the mop." And her daddy saying, "Mavis, when are we eatin'?" "Well, Ray, you see me. I can't let go. Well, fix yourself somethin'. Emilu, fix your father somethin' to eat." And Emilu saying under her breath, "This family is nuts," and thinking that for a grown-up man her father was as helpless as Barrelhead, who had to have something dumped in his dish. How come you could call yourself fully growed up, enough to have half of your hair done gone, and couldn't slide a piece of cheese into some bread?

"I ain't gonna never get married," she said. "I double-dog guarantee it I won't."

"Suit yourself," said her mother.

"I double-dog guarantee if I did I wouldn't put nothin' up in jars. It like to ruin ever summer there is."

"Watch your tongue, Emmy," her father said.

What with living through all the fury of canning, half the time she would go what somebody present would call too far and get sent from the table before dessert. Now that her grandfather was here for the summer, her mother cut her eyes to him as Emilu rose. "I hate to have your grandfather see you like this."

"He'll have to get used to it," Emilu said. "Ever thing around here ends up I did it."

She went to her room and lay on her bed with her feet against the headboard. Without turning over she could reach underneath and ease out the box that held her secret things. On the lid she had written: "Keep out or die." She opened it on her stomach and went through all its contents. A large dead June bug, a stick of teaberry gum, and a valentine that pictured a fluffy iced cake and was inscribed underneath: "You are the icing on my cake." On the back was printed: "I could devour you" and below, "Guess who" with a series of question marks. She had thought it came from Alma, but Alma said no, it must be a boy. She reviewed the possibility with horror and delight. She tore the gum in half and chewed out the sweet of it to make up for dessert.

Later on, she heard her grandfather moving the dresser around in his room. She got up and went to him. He had pushed it back into the place where it belonged.

He looked at her from where he stood by the window. "That woman muddies up my mind."

"You mean Mama?" she asked.

"I don't recall her," he said. "Was she here before?"

Emilu nodded.

"Well, she muddies my mind. Some women clear things. Your grandma . . . she did."

"What about me, Grandpa?"

"You clear things, little woman."

Her throat filled with pride.

"I been tryin' to get it straight."

She thought at first he meant who everyone was. But then she saw he meant the thing that had happened once. She heard her mother coming down the hall and slammed the door. She went and sat on the bed. "We gotta think about it harder."

He watched her in despair.

"Today is good," she said, coaxing him. "No rain. The sun is shinin'. The wind ain't blowin'."

He dropped into the chair before her. He hunched his head deep into the cave of his shoulders.

She sat and willed him to remember, holding her breath in as long as she could, plunging from one breathful into another.

"Little daughter . . . "

She sat stone-still and waited.

"There's a kinda mist . . . but I see a well . . . "

Still she waited. Then she said softly, as if she stroked a bird, "You already saw that, Grandpa." She waited again. "I got it for you."

He turned to look at her deeply. "You got it locked up tight? You won't fergit?"

She shook her head. "I got it."

She slung the hair from her eyes to see the things in his face. "Was it a real long time ago?"

"I reckon. It gits so it don't hardly matter when. It gits in your head and it don't hardly matter when it was. It's like it was in your blood," he said. "It's like it was always there."

There was pain in her chest from slowing her breath.

He began at last, "There comes a singin' in and outa my mind."

"I heard you singin' some in the night."

"It gits lost somewhere."

She smoothed his spread with a freckled hand. "It don't have to get lost with me to listen. I remember ever tune I ever heard, I guarantee. Words too." She waited for him. "Is it got some words to it, Grandpa?"

"I can't hardly say. I hear the tune, the way it went . . . "

She swung her feet and then she made them stop. "Maybe if you was to shut your eyes like it was dark."

He stared at her fiercely from under his wild brows. She could see in his eyes how it was he sailed his mind like a kite on a string and the two of them watched it soar above the house. He was seeing her now as if she was the string that he wouldn't let go.

"I hear a kinda beat like a heartbeat in the ground. I hear it but I feel it."

"What is it?" she said.

"It was turnin' red."

"And singin'?" she said.

His mind caught in the branches of the sycamore behind him.

"And singin', Grandpa?"

He was caught. He was lost.

She was waiting and wishing the tree frogs would shut up their racket for once. Barrelhead the dog began to bark at the squirrels. The bus, in the distance, had almost made the hill. At last she said, "Grandpa?"

His eyes had never left her face.

"Do you think you might a dreamed it?"

"No! No! It happened. Don't never say that again . . . Just hold on to what I give you. Are you doin' that, Mother?"

"I got it ever bit."

Sometimes he seemed to think that she was her grandmother, whom she had never known. Sometimes she seemed to be his daughter, Aunt Lou, her father's sister whose name was part of her own. She was afraid to ask. She wanted him to have her whichever way he would.

Slowly, very slowly his eyes lost light and seemed to recede beneath the crag of his brow. A dark, baffled look came over his face. "I lost it," he said.

They sat together, grieving, hearing the guineas gone to roost in the tree.

"I lost it," he said. Over the hill the train hit the bridge with a mourning cry and beat along the trestle and echoed in the hollow. She went out and crossed the road and climbed the hill. If a bus came by beneath she liked to practice her aim and pitch a rock at its roof. There was no bus in sight. It was maybe too late. She slithered down the hill to the tracks and walked a rail. It was cold as winter ice. She had learned how to skip along the rail and never fall. She skipped to a killdeer sitting on the track and flipped a rock to make him fly. She used to put nails where the train would make them flat. Her father said it was illegal. Now she felt a mingling of yearning and defiance. In the failing light she found a lid from a snuff can tossed between the ties. She laid it on the rail and willed the train to change it into something shining that had never been before.

After supper was over she went to her room. She lay on her back with her head at the foot to keep from going to sleep, legs perfectly straight, staring into the dark. She listened to the silence in her grandfather's room. She probed her own mind for the memory he sought, thrusting to the darkness and beyond to where it lay. Then the night opened like a hole in a gunny sack and covered her head. In a moment she slept.

But she woke in the dark to the sound of his song. She lay still and listened. It was almost her dream. She got up and tiptoed to his door.

His singing was strange. It was not any song she had ever heard before. It had no words, just his voice, a little cracked, humming, calling the notes, as if he were lulling her back into sleep. She rubbed her eyes awake and listened intently with her ear to the door. She hummed beneath her breath until the tune was in her head. Then she slipped back to bed and sang it to herself till she had it for good. She sang it to the train and it answered her back as it skimmed the rails, making something shining for her in the dark.

The next day after lunch her mother called her to the kitchen to pick up the clean clothes and put them away.

"Emilu, I wish you'd stay away from those tracks. I knew a woman caught her foot in them once, and along came the train."

"What happened?"

"What happened! She got killed, that's what."

"Did she get it caught where the rails got hitched or under the rail or under the tie?"

"Now, how would I know? She didn't live to tell us."

"I bet she was wearin' shoes . . . I wouldn't have on shoes."

Her mother left the room with the towels. Emilu called out, "Was she kin to us?"

"No, she wasn't kin. Nobody kin to us would do a crazy thing like that."

"If she wasn't kin to us I bet it never happened. Somebody made it up to scare people offa trains."

Her mother appeared in the doorway. "Emilu, it's time you grew up to your age."

"I ain't got the slightest idea what that means." She looked at her toes and the bottoms of her feet.

She went out to the barn and stared a hen in the eye and shooed the red one off her nest. She took one of the three tan-colored eggs and put it in her pocket and whistled from the doorway. After a while she walked behind the sycamore tree and pulled a leaf and laid it on the ground and broke the egg into it neatly. She knelt and touched the sulphur half-moon with the tip of her tongue. Then she called to Barrelhead to come and get it.

She went looking for her grandfather and found him asleep beneath the sugarberry tree. She sat down beside him.

She watched him sleep, his white hair stirring in the breeze. Crickets were jumping from the grass to brush his great brown hand that hung from the arm of the wicker chair. He was the oldest person she had ever known, and at the same time he was like a little baby that needed a mother. Nobody but herself would pay him any mind. Her mother seemed to think he was too much trouble just to have at the table, and now she let Emilu take his breakfast to his room. And her father never talked to him hardly at all. They talked around him at the table like he wasn't there. She began to sing softly the song she had heard him making in the night. She sang it over and over again till after a while it seemed to be her song for singing him asleep. He woke up and listened with his eyes half-closed. Then he shut them again and she thought he'd drifted off. But in a moment he said, "It was a woman done the singin'. It was like I was dreamin'. But when I come to she was singin' for real."

She listened in wonder. "Was it Grandma done the singin'?"

"No . . . no. But the moon was the brightest I ever seen."

He went to sleep again.

Her mother came to look at him and shake her head. "If it starts to rain I want that wicker chair inside."

"Mama," said Emilu, "can't you see he's asleep!"

"Well, I see that, Emilu. I don't need to be told. But if he's here for the summer we'll have to have things understood."

"I ain't got the slightest idea what that means."

"Never mind what it means. But I wish you wouldn't hang around him all the time."

"First it's the tracks and now it's Grandpa. There is more things around that I ain't got permission than there is I can do."

"Watch your tongue, Emilu."

Emilu stuck out her tongue and crossed her eyes to see it.

She had her supper and just before dark while they sat around the table she climbed the hill. The dark rails were now almost the color of the ground. They were like velvet ribbons you could hardly see. She skipped along one till she came to the shining round disc that caught light from the sky. The lid from the snuff can was like silver money and thin as thin. She picked it up and kissed it again and again.

She heard a mewing sound and turned to see that Barrelhead had followed her. He could sound like a cat enough to fool a kitten. "Go back," she commanded. "Barrelhead, go back." He sat down at once, blinking his eyes into the risen moon. Finally he turned and slunk away up the hill. "And don't you go blabbin' on me," she called.

Then she was walking the rail in moonlight, treading its silver. To make her free, in her mouth she held the silver disc with its faint snuff taste of honey and spice. Free of growing up, whatever it was.

She heard in the distance the sound of the train. It was calling to her like the bird in the corn. She was nearing the trestle. Deep in the iron her bare feet knew the yielding and tremor. The hollow below her was faintly in bloom. She walked straight on as she stepped to the bridge and boarded the trestle. The rails sang out. Around the curve toward her the great beast hurtled. She saw the trees ashen in its aureole of light. It sprang to the trestle. The white rails stammered. The churning of wheels. And then the glory of the shining rails.

Sucked into thunder, she turned and ran. Buried in thunder, running in terror, reaching the end, dropping to the gully to dwell forever in the house of thunder. She was rolling over, naked to the storm. Her heart was drowned, her life dissolving in the roar of the wheels.

She came to rest at the bottom of the gully. She floated over the world like foam. The frogs came back, tremulous, halting, then mounting a tenor of sad betrayal, then screaming as they remembered their song. She lay very still, and after a while she pitched her trembling voice to theirs. She could not tell if she made a sound. But beneath the moon she heard the singing in the well. She herself was in the well and heard the voice spilling down. For a moment she thought that she was dead, stone cold train-dead.

The cry rose inside her: If I got killed nobody could help. I'm the onliest one there is knows about the well. Not even Grandpa remembers it now.

She got up slowly and clawed her way through vines and frogs. At the top she found the silver round still clamped in her teeth. She took it out and buried it beneath a rock . . .

Her father saw her in the hall. "What happened to you?"

"I fell down."

He looked her over and sighed. "You all right?"

"Sure."

He opened his bedroom door and went in.

She stopped outside her grandfather's room and listened for a time to his gentle snore. And through the door she whispered to him: "Grandpa, I outraced a train."

Then she undressed and lay down to sleep. And the thunder shook her and shook her bed. She lay on her back and crushed the pillow to her face and choked and sobbed. I almost died, God. You 'most let me die. And God said, What got into you, Emilu? And Emilu said, I wish I knew.

In the night a rising wind was raking the leaves, and she covered her head to shut it out. She knew that tomorrow he would be caved in with everything in him slipped off somewhere.

In the morning he was desolate, hollow-eyed.

She became after that a watcher of weather. Fearful, she would sniff the damp in the air. When the wind hunkered down in the hollow, flinging the leaves, drumbeating the panes with fingers of rain, in another year she would have dashed through the trees, clarion with joy until they called her to shelter. Now she despaired, prowling in the hallway outside his room, gliding in to coax, "Don't worry, Grandpa. It won't last long."

But the rain ran down through the fissures in the bank to fill the bowl, and the house was a boat aground in the shallows. The pale moon floated its face in the yard for half the night. The geese honked curses from their dry retreat in a hollow oak. The watchdog guineas, gray and drenched, sat high on the branches above her window and warned of the wind in querulous tones. Below them, the tree frogs screeched their dominion of the sodden world — till daylight came.

She stole in softly with his plate of breakfast. He lay in bed. "Eat it hot, Grandpa. It will help you remember."

She sat brooding over him, warm with her tenderness, smoothing his cover. "Grandpa, there is a whole heap a little things I got locked in my mind. About the well and the singin' and the lady and all." She let her eyes stroke his bulky form. "Some other things too. All we got to do is get it together."

"I don't recollect a damn thing today."

"I could sing you the song."

"Give me the box, little woman." He pointed to it in the corner of the room.

She brought the box and took off the lid. He sat up and propped the pillow behind him. Then he drew from the box his uniform jacket and inched one arm into a sleeve. It was too small to cover more than half his chest.

"Did it shrink?" she asked.

He shook his head.

"You musta had it a long time ago."

He thought of it, frowning, with some surprise. "I don't recall."

"It's got real nice pretty buttons sewed on." Then she fed him some of the cereal. He ate it thoughtfully from her spoon.

"Little daughter," he said, "you got pretty ways."

"That ain't the general opinion around here."

"It's mine," he said.

He drank a little milk. "I think that woman out there wants me to leave."

"You mean Mama?"

"I don't recall her," he said.

"She ain't got such a crush on me neither, I guarantee."

They brooded together. He pulled the jacket a little more across his chest.

She swallowed on the words. "If you was to leave I wouldn't have nobody here."

He thought of it, his blue eyes circling the room. "You gonna help me, little mother. You gonna help me git it back."

She got up and closed the door and sat down again. She began to sing him softly the song of the well. He listened intently, then he hummed it to himself, breaking into a croon, his voice rising and sinking. His voice seemed to listen. And she listened with it, falling into its dream.

One day she brought his breakfast and he wasn't in his room. She put it down and waited. When he didn't return she tried the bathroom down the hall. The door was standing open. He was not inside. Her heart was in her throat. She closed the door to his room so her mother wouldn't see his breakfast on the tray. She searched for him among the trees in the hollow, with Barrelhead before her yipping at the squirrels. She looked into the corn and the wagon shed. She found him at last in the field beyond the corn on the bank of a ditch looking into the stream. He was still in his brown cotton flannel robe, with the box for the uniform beneath his arm. His white hair was like something silver in the sun. She was so glad to find him that she almost cried.

He looked up bewildered when he saw her beside him. His face was flushed in the sun. "It ain't the well," he said.

It was not an easy thing to get him back inside the house when no one was around.

After that she knew she had to think of something more than just remembering what he gave her. He hadn't told her anything new for some time. She felt him growing empty like he was hollowed out or something. She felt her mother just about to say he was crazy and maybe couldn't stay. And she felt herself sometimes like to break in two with holding off her mother and holding on to him.

Sometimes she almost got to wishing she was older, but then it scared her to look back and see how she was different at the first of the summer. Just with minding your own business, just treading water, things got dumped on you that you maybe couldn't handle any way but growing up. She thought it was enough to make you cuss out loud. And as soon as this was over she was backing up. But it was taking all she had and then some more to help him now. She had to get him what he wanted and then he could come back every summer of her life. Or they could live somewhere else, just the two of them together.

So she lay on her bed with her feet against the wallpaper, adding to the smudge she had already made. "I hate them rotten yellow roses," she said and stomped one with her heel.

One morning she climbed the hill and dropped down to the rock where she had buried the snuff lid the train had flattened thin. She sat on the rock and crossed her freckled legs and held the lid in her mouth. She thought she would maybe chop her hair off at the roots and give her mother a fit. And then she was crying and she didn't know why.

It was almost noon. She was getting hungry but she wouldn't go home. She sucked the lid in her mouth and thought of dipping snuff and spitting in a can, the way a black woman down the road would do, who took her spitting can with her wherever she went . . . Emilu spit into the weeds and cried.

And finally it came to her she knew about a well that used to be in a field a long way down the road. She had been there once when her daddy had bought a hound for himself. She had a drink from it then and the water had tasted like a mouth of ditch water with scum thrown in. Her father said not to worry, it was good to drink. But Emilu had thought, You coulda sure fooled me.

And now it seemed to her a last desperate hope. She could find the place. She could head straight back to any place she'd ever been. Like a cat, her father said. "We could put Emilu in a sack and dump her off down the road. She'd turn up the next day. Melissa you can turn around once and she's lost. Not Emilu."

I got to use everything I got, which ain't all that much. She wiped her eyes on her shirt and hid the snuff lid again.

It was hard work telling him about the well. He didn't seem to listen to what she said. She seemed to be telling it all to herself. When she had finished he sat leaning over with his head in his hands.

"Grandpa, I guarantee it wouldn't hurt none to look."

He got up and went to the corner for the box and put it under his arm. "I'm ready, little daughter."

At first she was too surprised to speak. Then she said, "We gotta take that bus and we ain't got time to make it today. We gotta wait till tomorrow."

Tears sprang to his eyes.

She went to him and pulled him down into the chair. She smoothed and patted his hair like silk. "Grandpa, you got real pretty hair. It's real real pretty, I'm tellin' you. It ain't no time at all till tomorrow gets here . . . Don't go mentionin' the bus. There is some folks around like to mess up your plans."

She found his peanuts on the dresser and they ate some together.

She had a little money for the bus. There was her grandmother on her mother's side who sent her a five-dollar bill every birthday came around. That way you could get it figured into your affairs. It had come in June and she hadn't busted into it yet. It would be enough for one way but not for coming back. She slipped into her father's drawer and got some from the box in the corner at the back. She knew it would be the whole thing come down upon her if he found it out. Like she had robbed a train.

The bus would come by a little after two, but she got him ready early after lunch was over. She brushed and combed his hair and aimed his eyebrows in the right direction. He wanted to take along the box with his uniform, but she brought him around to taking just the jacket instead.

She put on her black leather sandals and her Easter dress that had the jacket with the braid. She thought to take corn muffins left from lunch and stuff them into the pockets of her dress. And when her father left in the truck and her mother was sitting out in back in the swing the way she did after lunch, she took her grandfather's hand and led him out to the road. She walked him down around the bend so that no one looking out could see them from the porch, and she pushed him into the shadow of an oak.

The air was empty, the way it is on summer afternoons when it's making up its mind if it intends to rain. It seemed to her the bus was a long time in coming. Then she heard it struggling with the hill. It was bearing down upon them. She stepped out to hail it and it came to a stop. She coaxed him up the steps. She had her money ready. She would not look around for fear of seeing someone who would know her. But when they were seated just behind the driver she did look down the aisle. The bus was almost empty. Three blacks, a woman and two men, were sitting in the rear. A white man halfway down appeared to be asleep.

She patted her grandfather's arm and smiled at him. His eyes were grave and trusting. She hooked her Sunday sandals on the driver's seat and stared at the back of his head and ears and tried to tell if he was kind and if he would stop where she said to stop.

He stopped the bus exactly where she pointed and never asked her a thing. But she saw him looking hard at the uniform.

There was a haze on the fields. She took her grandfather's hand and led him down a little dirt road between some burdock trees. And then the road ended and they were out in the open. She climbed through a fence and held the wire up for him. But he just stepped over with no trouble at all. There were cows ahead, mostly Jerseys she saw. But a Guernsey bull raised his head as they passed and looked at her hard. She looked back hard and kept on going, though she was scared inside. Insects were chirring like crazy in the heat.

She found a spot beneath a tree and made him sit down. She

folded his uniform and put it beside him. "I gotta find it, Grandpa. It might take a minute." She took off running.

She explored every hollow and behind every hillock. She almost panicked. She had been so sure it was there in the field . . . And then through a section of broken fence she found it. She went running back for him and coaxed him to it.

There it was in the weeds, a square of old boards greened over with moss. She tried to lift it. "It's under there, Grandpa. You lift it up. It's too heavy for me."

He stood looking down at it with deep concentration. His eyes were blue pinpoints back under his brows.

She wasn't sure that he understood. "It's the well, Grandpa. I found it. See. You take off the top and look down inside . . ." She scanned the sky for him. "It's a real good day. No wind or rainin'. It's a real good day for rememberin' things. I can remember even bein' a teeny baby. I can remember the farthest back I ever done."

He stood without moving.

Now she was pleading. "Take off the top, Grandpa. It'll be just fine." She knelt in the weeds and patted the boards.

Slowly he approached and stood looking down at her moving hands.

"Lift it up, Grandpa."

He stooped and grasped the edge of one board and threw the lid back with a crash. She fell over backward into the weeds. Then she got to her knees and peered into the well. A smell of decaying vegetation rose. She looked up at his face in the sky above her. He seemed bewildered. "Sit down with me, Grandpa."

He stared out across the field and stirred and half turned. She thought he could leave. She stood up and took his hand and pulled him down beside her. She was praying to herself: God, you gotta help me get it goin'. The hardest thing there is is to get somethin' goin' that ain't started yet.

She picked up a stone and dropped it into the well and heard it strike the ground. She turned to him a stricken face. "It used to be fulla water. I had a drink out it once . . . It's done dried up, I reckon . . . And it's got fulla dirt."

But his face was changing. She could not tell what it meant. He said to her, "Little daughter . . . you gonna give me what you got saved up. You hear?"

"It's a dried-up well."

"It don't matter about the water." He was impatient now. "Give me what all you got."

She held on to the muffins in each pocket of her dress. "I got a lady singin' and a well and a beatin' in the ground and somethin' red. I got the moon." She began to sing the well song but her voice was crying. She didn't want to cry, but her voice came out crying and she had to stop. "I got you said it was the best thing ever happen . . ."

"Not at first," he said.

"How come you told me it was?"

"Not at first," he said, shaking his head from side to side. Suddenly he grabbed the jacket and threw it on his back and drew it close around his throat. "It was some kinda . . . It musta been that war . . ."

"What war was it, Grandpa?" She tried to think of the wars she had heard about in school but they all ran together and she couldn't help.

He stroked his head.

"What was they fightin' about, Grandpa?" She had to keep him talking. The worst was when he stopped. "I wouldn't a fought 'less they give me a reason."

"They give one," he said. "I fergit what it was."

He pulled the uniform around his throat and put it to his lips and smelled of it.

"They was runnin' through trees and outa trees. I heard shootin' in the trees. I heard Jake gittin' hit, and I turn and saw blood comin' outa his throat. Like he was tryin' to tell me somethin', 'stead a words it was blood. Me and him kep' runnin' and then he wan't there. And then I fell down and I seen I had Jake's blood all over my side . . . It wan't his, it was mine, but I didn't know it. I thought it was his. I run on further and I fell again. I fell into somethin' was a hole . . . was a well."

She heard thunder in the hills. He lifted his head. He heard it too. Now, she thought, he's gonna dry up like the well is done dried. But the words were still there. "I hear runnin'. I hear runnin'. Feet poundin' the ground. Like a heartbeat in the ground. And like all at once the sky goes away . . ."

He stopped.

"What was it, Grandpa? Did you pass clean out?"

He put the jacket to his lips. "No . . . no. It was the top for the well." He reached out and stroked it with his fingers. "She covered me up."

"Who did, Grandpa?"

He shook his head.

"Who did it, Grandpa? You gotta think real hard."

"You recollect your mother used to cover you up? 'Fore you was good asleep?"

"It wasn't Grandma. It wasn't her. It was back in that war."

"She used to sing you asleep."

She stared at him in despair. "Not Grandma . . ." She lay back on the ground.

"That woman . . . in the war."

She heard him from where she lay and was afraid to move.

"Feet was poundin' all around me." He began to moan and tore the uniform away and threw it onto the ground. "I could hear the shoutin'. And she was settin' on top a me. On top a the well. Right on top a the well. And she was singin'. It was a song. I never heard nothin' like it." He began to sing the song, at first a whisper, then loud. She could hear it way down in the pit of her stomach. And she heard how the cows were listening to it in the field.

"Then she stopped," he said. He began to cry softly.

I'm a willin' to grow up some, God, if it takes it . . .

He grew calm and wiped his eyes on the back of his hand. "They was askin' did she see me. They was talkin' foreign words, but I knew what they said . . . When you is settin' hunched up underground in the dark . . . in the wet . . . in the blood . . . and they is huntin' you down like a rabbit . . . it don't matter what kinda words. I am sayin' it don't matter what kinda words."

Then she saw him lean across the well and fall in. But not fall. He climbed inside.

She got to her knees and looked down upon him where he sat with his head against the sides and his white hair all speckled with sticks and fern. She thought it might be that he was going to die. She had never seen somebody die before, and she was aching all over with wanting him to live.

She heard him saying, "She was singin' in the dark. I never heard nothin' like it. They come back a dozen times. They was huntin' me down. But she was singin' on the well and they never look inside."

She heard his voice growing into a song. "I was young to be dyin'. I ain't grew up, and I wanted it like a drink a cold water when your tongue is dry. I seen how it was I been wastin' the world. I ain't half look at things in the field or the road or sky. I ain't half smell the hay in the rain . . . I ain't love a woman. I seen 'em in doorways and walkin' pretty, but I ain't love one. I wanted a woman and the chil'ren she give. Lyin' with her at night, gittin' up at day . . . I wanted gittin' old."

She heard the cows lowing, coming close with their lowing. Bees sang in the trees.

Wanted getting old?

But it wasn't over. For he turned his face upward and into her own. His eyes were seeking something beyond her face, beyond her help. "Long time in the dark 'fore she open me up. I thought it was sun. It was moon shinin' on me the brightest I seen. It was like her face was up in the moon lookin' down at me. It was like I been given it all right there, the rest a my life poured into that hole in the ground where I was . . . I couldn't hardly bring myself to come up then, 'cause I had it all there. I reckon I was 'fraid if I lived it out it might not be that good."

"Was it?" she said, not knowing what he meant or what she asked or why.

But it seemed to be gone. All she could see was his head sunk down and the sticks and fern and the leaves in his hair.

He stirred. "Did you git it?" he cried.

She swallowed and nodded down into the well. "I got it, Grandpa."

"It's slippin', a'ready slippin'. You got it, little daughter?"

"I got it, Grandpa." Inside, she was crying, not knowing what she had.

"That's good," he said. "It's yours. You keep it."

Keep what? Keep what?

Going back was hard. The sky was changing, going gray at the edges, then gray on top. By the time they were back at the road it was raining. She got him to sit on the side in the grass. She took off her jacket and put it over his head. The uniform she buttoned inside his shirt, but he didn't seem to care about it any more. She felt it was raining down inside of her. Counting on her fingers, she guessed it would be a good five hours before the bus would return.

But long before that, her father's car lights picked them out through the mist.

"Emilu," said her mother in the front seat, turning, "I would expect from you a little more judgment."

"Shut up!" she cried, coming out of the rain. "I was helpin' Grandpa. I'll never tell what it was. Not if all my teeth rot out! Not if you lock me up forever!"

But he was the one they locked away . . .

Whatever it was he found in the well, sometimes she wished she could lock it up in the box she kept beneath her bed. A thing you have to keep in your mind, it gets shrunk up, or else it grows the way you do and blurs like a lantern held too close till, like it or not, you look away. But after a dozen summers were gone, it must have been when her child was born, she heard the cry of the thing they had found. She heard the singing inside of her.

Money Man

Let it be recorded that the owner of a metal detector is a dreamer. The dream words in the catalog are made for him. Danny pulled the dream words over his head like the green stocking cap he always wore. Then one night he played long, dreaming songs on his guitar, and in the morning he took it down and sold it. It was like selling his voice and hands.

But he figured that with the money he could order the Bounty-Finder from the catalog, and, with money he found with it, buy back his guitar, or maybe buy another that was even better, and still go on finding money forever. For a Bounty-Finder dreamer knows, he knows that money has been dropped or lost or hidden in the ground or in the leaves or in the roots of grass and trees or in the beds of flowers, in the ditches and the drains, and that it goes on being dropped or lost or hidden without end.

Danny thought a lot about money, but not in the usual way of thinking: that money is for going places, buying things. Besides, he had his government pension for his crippling — the right side of him out of line and lower than the left. (And who knows how or when it happened? It was there.) Two days a week he worked in a car wash. And he had his little house, weathered, tumbled, leaning to one side like himself, but it served him. And he was thirty-three, as best he knew, a time when things are settled one way or another, especially with one side of him lower than the rest. No, with Danny the money simply was for finding. It was for making a day come alive and green. It was for making him a little one-day future. Tomorrow he would hear the gentle humming shift its note to the shrill money song. And of course it was for buying back his guitar.

So he took his Bounty-Finder to the schoolyard and the park, the best places to look. The schoolyard was best of all. The children had lost lunch and candy money there for the last fifty years and cried and forgotten. It wasn't like taking it away from any of the children who crowded around him, eyes big with envy and admiration. It was all in the past. Maybe the money had belonged to their fathers when they themselves were little. Sometimes a boy would claim it, saying, "My father says he dropped it, no kidding, right there." And the others, who liked Danny, chanted, "Prove it, prove it!" But whenever a child said, "I lost my lunch money there," Danny looked him in the eye and asked for the date on the face of the coin. And if the boy could tell him he'd give it back. All the children memorized the dates on their coins, because Danny would give them back if you told him true.

Danny hadn't ordered the kind of detector that rules out junk. That kind costs more. Besides, he liked the junk — the metal buttons, the paper clips, the dog tags, the pieces of foil. He stored them in the left-side pocket of his jacket. The money he put into the right-hand side. There was something more secure about the side that was crippled. Sensations were keener on the whole of that side. A thief could pick the left pocket and Danny might not know. But when someone touched his right side ever so lightly, he felt it in his heart and the marrow of his bones. Like brushing the strings of his guitar it was. At the end of his day he emptied his pockets into two cardboard boxes, one for money, one for junk. Except that it wasn't really junk to Danny. It was pieces of the world that he wanted to save. And as for the money, he washed and polished each piece till it shone. He dreamed of finding a golden coin.

To the children he was hero; he was Money Man. They spent their play periods watching him hunt. Sometimes he let them hold the detector in their hands. "Danny, how much money do you find in a day? How much money in a month?" "Danny, where do you keep it?" "Danny, what are you gonna buy with all that money?"

"A guitar," he said.

He found that in the evenings, when he always used to play it, he missed his guitar; but after a while he didn't mind so much. He could stroke the air with his fingers and dream the vibration up his arm and down into his hands and up into his throat and make up the songs the way he used to do. It took just a little extra thought to do it. The vibration in his hand when he'd played his guitar was a lot like holding the detector in his hand.

Still, he was sad about losing the guitar. He said he wasn't sad but the songs grew sad. He sang about the dead bird he had found among the leaves – it was autumn now – and the gray squirrel caught in the grating to the drain. He sang about the rain when the children were not allowed to come out and watch. He never, however, sang about himself. There was nothing to say or know about himself. Except that the children called him Money Man and when he left the school the dogs would follow. They seemed to come for blocks, for miles around, barking to one another, "Danny's going home." If he turned he could see them running in a pack, nipping one another but all in fun.

He didn't really mind. He even liked it. When he came to his crippled house, he opened the door and they followed him in. He led them down the hall and straight out the back where they yipped and chased the squirrels, while he circled the house and re-entered by the front. His old brown setter, whose name was Stretch, would be hiding for his life underneath the bed. And now he would emerge. And Danny would talk to him about the day. Then after supper, propped up on his bed with Stretch lying under it, he would strum the air and sing about the day, while the dog moaned and coughed and beat his ragged tail on the springs of the bed.

It's the simplest sort of thing to describe what happened and the way it happened. But to tell about the difference it made in his life would require a better song than Danny could make.

He was crouching in the schoolyard close to the walk. The detector was shrilling. He was probing the earth with the tip of the screwdriver he carried in his belt for the purpose. School was over for the day and the children had gone home. So it startled him when someone stopped on the walk beside him. He saw the little soft shoes, soft and gray as a squirrel. He looked up to find the teacher they called Miss Tracy. He had seen her from a distance. He knew the children loved her. In the strangest sort of way he came to hate the teachers they hated and to like the ones they did. And that was the way it was. So already without knowing her or seeing her up close he had liked Miss Tracy. And now she stood before him, the prettiest girl he had ever seen. As if she had touched him on his crippled side, he felt her in his heart and the marrow of his bones. She was standing with the sunlight shining through the ends of her short brown hair and tipping it with gold. And her eyes were golden and so hidden with lashes that they seemed like autumn leaves he uncovered in the grass. Just to look at her softness was to hold it in his hand. He dropped his eyes to her little gray shoes.

He knelt at her feet till she asked him uncertainly in a sweet, girl's voice: "Do you think . . . will that thing find a key, do you think?"

He was drowning in her voice. It was two notes struck together on the strings of his guitar. He looked up without seeing her.

She hesitated, then went on. "You see, I lost a key somewhere by the walk. I thought if you could find it I'd be very grateful."

"Where?" he asked, his voice breaking.

Her laugh was uncertain. "I don't know. But I'm sure it's by the walk. It would be that side, the side you're on. I tried to find it, but there's so many leaves." She finished shyly, "I thought if you had the time . . ."

"I'll look," he said quickly. He did not rise, because he didn't want her to see that he was lower on one side. The children didn't mind but he thought that she might.

"I'd really be grateful." She waited for a moment. "If you find it you could leave it at the principal's office." Her shoes went away down the walk and then turned. "My name is Laura Tracy in case you find it."

"I'll look," he said so low that she couldn't have heard.

After that he hunted for the key with a total dedication. He marked the yard that bordered the walk into sections with a sturdy piece of branch and methodically searched them in the afternoon sun. He found a dog tag, a strip of chrome, and a nickel and a dime. It wasn't till he gave up and tried the other side of the walk that he came upon a key hidden in the grass beneath a sycamore leaf. It might not be the one but then again it might, it looked so

new. It was a thick, firm key with a green string knotted in the hole
at the top. An important-looking key that might unlock a school-
room door, or a cabinet where supplies were kept, or a house.

It was Friday afternoon and the school was locked, and he
wouldn't see Miss Tracy again till Monday. He put the key in the
money pocket of his jacket, and on the way home with the dogs at
his heels he stopped at a telephone booth and looked up her name
in the book. He saw that she lived about six blocks away. He stood
for a while beside the telephone, fingering the key in his money
pocket and looking out at the dogs that were circling the booth. It
never occurred to him to telephone her. He had hardly ever used a
phone in his life. Phones made him uneasy.

In the morning full of autumn sun he skipped the car wash where
he usually went on Saturdays, and instead found Miss Tracy's
house. He took his metal detector with him in case he passed the
kind of ground, old and trampled, that looked like treasure. And
besides, when he held it, it gave him a reason to be leaning on one
side.

He stood on the sidewalk and looked at the number of the house
in the grass and then at the house painted white and the gray roof
the color of her shoes and the shrubbery in front that was crackling
with sparrows. He shifted the detector to his left-hand side and,
keeping his finger on the key in his pocket, he advanced to the
door. The sparrows scattered. He knocked for a while, then rang
the bell. Since it was Saturday she might be home. He waited a long
time, so long that the sparrows flew back into the bushes. He took
out the key and touched it to his face. Then, without having
thought of doing it before, he tried the key in the door. When it
turned in the lock he was not surprised. He thought that he had
known all along it was the key to her house. It had a warm, smooth
surface that was the way a key would feel that could open a house.
His own house had only a secret way of leaning on the door.

He pushed the detector out of sight behind a bush. Then he
opened the door before him and stood on the threshold, not seeing
much till his eyes grew accustomed to the dusk. He entered, and
what he saw was something he could sing about forever. The carpet
was golden like her eyes and the tips of her hair in the sun. And the

pieces of furniture, the sofa and the chairs, were covered with a cloth full of brown and yellow leaves. Most beautiful it was, like an autumn inside without any of the dust and the bare dead places and the gray stalks of goldenrod withered and spent. On the walls were scattered pictures as bright as butterflies. The room had a warm and wonderful smell. A long, deep smell like flowers that were saved and dried in the sun. But no, as he advanced, it was more like apples. But that could be from the bowl of them he saw on a table in the kitchen beyond.

To hold in the fragrance he went back and closed the door he had left wide open. Then he took off his shoes and stood in bare feet so as not to mar the carpet. It was soft as grass.

He stood for a time taking in the room — the clock on the mantel, the shining tables at each end of the sofa with silver lamps, the small glass animals beneath the lamps, the picture of sheep on the wall above them, the curtains like the foam the children could churn with their feet in the puddles.

Then he went very slowly into the room where she slept at night. Here again he walked on a soft and golden rug. But the cover on the bed was the color of a jaybird's wing. Beside the bed was a small child's rocker that was painted blue, and in the rocker was a small, stuffed bear with gold bead eyes and a smiling mouth sewn of purple thread.

He could not resist going to the rocker and stooping to set it in gentle motion. Then he turned to her dresser full of fragile objects he had never seen before. At one end was a picture of an older man and beside him a woman with a worn, sweet face. At the other end was a picture of two smiling girls with long, curling hair. One was Miss Tracy, smaller and younger, and the other was a girl that looked like her. He opened the drawer at the top of the dresser. It was shining inside with her delicate things. He closed it quickly, feeling warm and faint. Through the mirror he stared at the wall behind him. It was covered with a pattern of little white roses. They seemed to be climbing a trellis of gold. And in front of the flowers he could see the bed. It too was made of a golden metal, and it held all the blue like a lake in the sun.

He turned away to set the blue rocker again in motion. It rocked its shadow on the golden rug. The eyes of the bear swam with gold in the sun. He looked for a long time down at the bed. Then he took off his green knit cap and stuffed it into the pocket of his jacket. He knelt and took off the plastic jacket and folded it and placed it beside the bed. Then into the cold blue lake of the spread he lowered the right-hand side of his face, the side that knew singing and golden things. The cloth was cool and softer than moths that come at night. And kneeling like this, he could all at once remember a time long ago, before the county home where he lived as a child. The memory was dim. It was dark at the edges. But someone had held him. He was gently in motion. He was almost, almost hearing a song. The memory startled him, so new it was. But after a time he was not surprised. It must have lain for years in a corner of his mind, an old, old thing he hadn't found before.

Hearing the bark of a dog on the street, he was suddenly in terror lest she come in and find him. He sprang to his feet. He put on his jacket and tore the green cap away from his pocket. A coin fell and rolled on the golden rug. He snatched it quickly and left the room. His beating heart was a bird he had snared.

As he left the house he went into the kitchen, alive with sun and apple fragrance, and dropped the coin among the apples. He could not have told why he did such a thing. He locked the front door and thrust the key deep into his pocket.

He took to going to the house in the mornings when he knew that Miss Tracy would be at school. He always carried the detector with him and hid it in the shrubbery before he entered. It gave him a sort of courage to have it along. But as the days passed he didn't need the courage. It seemed to him almost as natural as eating to visit the house several times a week. It wasn't as if he went there to pry into her life. He made himself useful on each occasion. There were things about the house that she had left undone in her haste to be gone. Sometimes a towel in the bathroom had fallen to the floor. Sometimes it was her cereal bowl in the sink. It was almost the blue of the cover on her bed. It was rimmed with white daisies with golden centers. He washed and dried it carefully and set it in the window in the sunlight while he rinsed her drinking glass and rubbed it till it sparkled like a diamond in a ring. And in the evening he strummed his ghost of a guitar and sang about the little blue bowl in the sun. In his song it was the sky rimmed with bits of cloud.

The apples in the bowl he polished till they glowed. He liked to smell them and touch them to his face. Sometimes there were oranges like golden balls. Every day he washed them and left them gleaming in the window while he swept the kitchen.

He always went into the bedroom and set the bear to rocking in a gentle way. All the time that he was working in another room he felt the bear was waiting for him to come in and rock him. The golden bead eyes never minded him around. The smiling mouth was sewn a little crooked with the purple thread. And perhaps this was why he came to feel almost as if the bear were Danny.

Before he left the house he drew out of his pocket a washed and polished coin from the store of them he kept in the box at home. Each time he placed one in a different spot: on the kitchen counter beneath the blue bowl. On the mantel in the living room behind the clock, or among the glass animals beneath the lamp. And once between the rockers underneath the smiling bear. It was like leaving a part of himself. Or maybe even like planting a seed.

In the afternoons he hunted for money at the school. He saw Miss Tracy on the playground at times but she never came near. Sometimes she was playing games with the children. Once he had a glimpse of her skipping rope, while they laughed and shouted and clapped their hands. Her hair was dancing and glinting with gold. Then suddenly down through the sun came rain. And Miss Tracy clapped her hands to her hair and ran for the school while they all ran after her, screaming with glee and clapping their hands to their heads as well. He had never in his life been able to run. But now in his sleep he dreamed of running. He and Miss Tracy were running with the children. He knew all the ones in her second-grade class. He had learned their names. He had a special feeling when they were near, as if they were born to Miss Tracy and himself.

Working late, several times he saw her sailing down the street past the school on the bicycle she kept on her little back porch behind the kitchen. He saw it one morning and noticed that its chain was almost worn through. He tried to fix it with the screwdriver he always carried thrust into his belt, but it wouldn't do. He decided that tomorrow he would bring his tools. That afternoon when he saw her gliding past the grounds of the school he was cold with terror lest the chain should break. The detector was humming while his heart flew beside her beating like wings to enfold and hold her. From that moment on she belonged to him. No one had ever belonged to him before. The following morning he repaired the chain.

After that there were other things to be repaired. He left the tools at her house underneath the porch. He stopped the dripping of the kitchen faucet. The towel rack in the bathroom was loose at one end, and the screen on the back porch was coming unnailed.

One day when it was raining and the wind was fingering the trees like the strings of a guitar and brushing the ivy on the window pane, he turned on the lamp above her dresser. To see if it was working, he told himself, but really for the sake of himself and the bear. Then he noticed a slender gold chain that was broken in two. It was lying in a heap to one side of the worn, sweet face of the woman in the picture. In his bare feet he sat on the carpet with his tools around him to mend the broken link. And as he was mending it his penknife slipped and he cut his finger. His blood sprang and fell on the golden rug. At first he was paralyzed with horror. In a dream of grief he brought water from the kitchen to wash away the blood. He removed the most of it, but near the corner of the dresser was a spot that remained. The eyes of the bear were bright and accusing. When he left at last, no place in all the house would accept his coin.

Now the songs in the evening he sang no more. Nor could he go again to the school for money. He told himself that he could never return to her school or her house. He had hurt her house in some unspeakable, unforgivable way.

He stayed at home and mourned for a week. Then he went to the park for money. The days were growing into winter. He buttoned the plastic jacket up to his chin and pulled the knit cap down over his ears. The blackbirds were busy in the grass when he appeared and flew into the sky with a drumming of their wings and settled in the trees and watched him with resentment. He didn't belong there. In the evenings now he sang about the park and the feathers in the air and the leaves that were pasted like paper on the bench. And the crow that called down from a sycamore tree. But in the midst of his song the blue bowl would appear with its rim of clouds or the sky like a bowl with flowers at the edge. The words were all mixed, and his fingers ached with fingering the air. And Stretch was moaning like a sick old woman underneath the bed.

He went on mourning. The skies were gray. The money in the park sank deeper down into the ground out of sight and reach. He counted what he had in the cardboard box. And then one morning when the frost was on the grass, he put it all into the pocket of his jacket and went to her house and opened the door. It was such a relief to be there that he sank to the floor just inside the door while he took off his shoes. He put his head in the green knit cap back against the wall and smelled the warm fragrance and laughed to himself. After a while he got up and walked through the house, discovering it again with the deepest joy. He looked long and deeply at the pictures on her dresser. The faces belonged to him as never before. He took off his cap and then his jacket and knelt by the bed in the way that he had done the first time of all, and drowned the right side of his face in the blue. On the table by her bed was a letter she was writing. While he knelt he read it, murmuring the words. "Dear Sister," it said. Then it told about the children in her class at school. It talked about the house and how she loved it. "I'm saving my money for some china cups."

When he had finished he put on his cap and then his jacket and fingered the money he had placed in his pocket, and he rocked the bear. And then without wanting to he looked for the stain that his blood had made. It had disappeared, as if it had never been there at all. He couldn't believe it, and he wept for joy. And rejoicing, he walked again through the house, touching the things that had made him glad. He went to the kitchen to smell the apples.

All of a sudden the door was opened and shut again. He almost cried out. And then Miss Tracy was there before him. He was too astounded to speak or move. He watched her mouth open to scream and then close. She backed away from him into the living room and groped for the door with her hands behind her. Her golden eyes were wide and dark with a question. And then he saw how afraid she was.

He caught her fear as if she had flung it to him where he stood. They shared it as deeply as love is shared. And now, when finally she found the door, he could see that her body relaxed a little. And slowly the wildness of their terror drained. But they watched each other like hunter and hunted, and each was hunter and each was prey. The stalking and circling was in their eyes.

Finally, she said in a small, tight voice that was almost a whisper, "I've seen you before."

He reached in his pocket and pulled out the key. He held it up by the green string knotted in the hole at the top, to show that he had given up touching her things. It seemed she had never seen it before. Then her face remembered the walk where he knelt and her key that was hidden under all the leaves.

"You've been here before," she said to him slowly, as if she remembered, as if she had found the coins he'd left or the blue bowl washed or the chain repaired, as if it were all coming into one place in her mind at last.

He let her see that he placed the key on the table beside the apples. She watched him in a dream. Then he took from his pocket the coins he had brought from the cardboard box. They were knotted tightly in a piece of cloth. He stood leaning into himself on his crippled side and slowly untied the knot in the cloth. Then he turned and poured the coins beside the key. They smelled of apples. They were silver and gold.

He spoke for the first time. "They're for your cups."

He could see that she didn't understand his words. And that fear was clouding the gold of her eyes.

His own fear was gone. "I wouldn't hurt you. I love you." And as soon as he had said it he knew it was so and would always be so and was the truest thing that he had ever said.

She opened the door for him without a word. He found his detector in the shrubbery. And so he went away from her down her walk, past the sparrows in her fallen leaves, past the number of her house where it melted into her grass with the frost. The dogs came for blocks, for miles around, barking to one another, "Danny's going home."

The Healing

From where she lay in bed Mrs. Crane could see her grandson playing under the cottonwoods. Every day she lay there watching for him to come out after breakfast, watching for him to come out after dinner. And now that it was summer and the days were long he always came out after supper. Then she could see him running back and forth under the moving leaves, round and round the trunk of the largest tree as if he were pursued. Slipping, spilling through foaming sand, then riding, riding the lowest branch till the leaves were whipped to a froth of sound. Through the open window she could hear his merry shouts. And she listened to them with a still absorption as if they were meant for her.

It was morning now, almost eight o'clock, and her son Wayne came into her bedroom. He eased himself down to the foot of her bed and looked out with her at his racing child. He was a tall, bulky man with graying hair. The bedsprings whimpered under his weight. His face and neck were amber with sun. Even his eyes were stained with amber. His massive hand on the bedpost now was creased and spotted the color of rust. Since the death of his wife the year before, he too liked to look at the happy boy.

"He needs another boy to play with," he said now.

His mother shook her head above her still body. She rarely moved her swollen limbs because of the pain. "He doesn't need anything," she answered, but she did not take her eyes from the boy.

"How can he keep it up? He'll wear out." He smiled, for he did not think it.

"No," she said, for she did not think it either. But she did not smile.

They listened in silence, smelling the dust and the summer leaves. The fields beyond them waited for rain, but the drought was good for the haying now. And good for the boy who liked to play. He could shake the leaves till they sounded rain. In their grown-up innocence they could not tell if he were Davy Crockett or one of the cowboy stars he talked of . . . or if he were just himself, Davy Crane, a little six-year-old in blue jeans and white T-shirt and a leather belt that sparkled with varicolored glass like jewels. The belt had been a birthday present from his grandmother.

Her son got up from the bed, but he kept his eyes on the boy outside. "Feeling any better today?"

She shook her head above her still body, and he knew the gesture as if he had turned and seen it.

Then he rode out on his horse to the fields. Since the death of his wife he spent a great deal of time in the fields, often helping his hands with the work of haying, so that when he returned at sundown for supper he was tired out and sat on the porch. And then for a little while before he went to bed he watched his son playing under the cottonwoods. Sometimes he turned on the radio and listened to the news while he watched his son. Yet he rarely heard. It was good that the world went on with its business. But if the confident voice changed to music, then he sat while his soul was twisting inside him and tears stood in his eyes. Before his wife died, he had believed in God and in the mysterious goodness of life. Now he believed in the work and the fields and the night, in sleep.

Then he would stand up slowly, hating and loving the music, and call out to Davy, "Bedtime, son," and walk into the house and switch off the music with his great, broad hand. He would pause at his mother's door. "Good night, Mother." It was just a way of speaking, for she never had a good night. She never slept. Then he went to his own room where his wife dwelt at night. She dwelt in the rest of the house by day. Sometimes she met him at the edge of the field. When he entered his room he would bind his breath and undress in the dark and know her like a mist on the face of the moon. If she had not been waiting he could not have slept.

Mrs. Crane watched her grandson playing in the yard all morning. Then her son came in from the field for dinner. The black woman had walked down the graveled road in her strong bare feet with the silver coin chained to her ankle. She called the boy in from under the trees, and in a little while she brought in food on a tray and stood while the old lady ate it slowly. She always ate only a little because it was painful to move her arms. She ate just till the pain balanced her hunger, and then another mouthful that was never worth the pain. She did not like to be fed by someone else.

Then before the woman took away the tray, Mrs. Crane said in her plaintive voice, "Lou, there's a fly. It buzzes so . . . " And Lou took the swatter from the windowsill and stalked the fly in her strong bare feet.

"I don't see it, ma'am."

"You look. It's there." For the old lady liked to keep her a while. She liked to see the simple ease of her motion and the power in her arm. And it gave her pleasure to know that she ruled them for a little time. It made them seem in a way her own.

When the woman finally took away the tray, Mrs. Crane would turn just enough to see the strong black feet as they disappeared and the flash of the coin, which then like a mirror would flash in her mind, setting on fire the things she had been. The way she had been in the days of her youth. Her laughing mouth. Her strong round limbs to catch the heart of a man, running, running through the summer grass. Then she turned her eyes again to the window and watched for her grandson to reappear. Refreshed by food, he always played with a greater vigor.

He had played there now for an hour when he turned and ran into the house for something, an arrow or a ball. She heard him racing past her room. And when he hurried back she called to him, "Davy, come here," and turned her head above her still body to see him in the doorway.

He came in out of the dusky hall and stood by her bed. He was an obedient child. But it was a tightly coiled obedience, as if he must hold himself in check or his body-spirit would run away.

She looked at him with her bright old eyes. His face with its freckles was grimed and flushed, and sand drifted out of his sand-colored hair. "Come sit on my bed for just a minute."

"What for?" he said. But he did not really question it, because he had never understood anything that she wanted. She lived in another world. All her wants were conditioned by age and pain, all her words, her thoughts. He had never known age, and what he had known of pain was forgotten.

He came closer now and sat on the foot of her bed and looked out of the window at the cottonwood trees, as if he could see himself playing beneath them. So strong was his desire.

She sensed it and it gave her a kind of pleasure. "You can stay here just a minute with your old granny, can't you?"

He nodded briefly. He smelled to her of sand and leaves and sun. He glanced down into the pocket of his shirt and pulled out a leaf and then a cricket. He held it closer for her to see. Then he put it carefully back in his pocket and covered it up with the leaf again. "It's alive," he said, and his smile was the flash of the silver coin. She was running, running through the summer grass.

She measured her words in pinches of dust. "Your old granny has to stay here all day and all night . . . How would you like that?"

He looked at her with a small surprise, but he did not answer.

"How would you like that?" she said again.

He stirred on the foot of the bed. "I wouldn't like it."

She moved her head from side to side on the pillow, never taking her eyes from his small boy's face, the stub of a nose that was pink with sun, the pale damp hair that was almost white. "I don't like it either."

He did not answer. She could feel his desire to be under the trees. She moved her eyes down his white T-shirt, now smudged with dirt. "That's a pretty belt, Davy. Who gave it to you?"

"You did," he said in surprise. "Don't you remember?"

"Yes," she said. "I just wanted to see if you did. Do you like it?"

He nodded, and he stuck his small thumb behind one of the jewels.

"Come closer, Davy. I want to see it."

Obediently he edged toward her on the bed. Painfully she reached out a swollen, crooked finger and touched a blue stone like a sapphire. "I'm glad you like it." Then she said, "Of course I had to send your father to get it. I couldn't go to town and get it myself."

She put her hand on his warm bare arm. The swollen joint had trapped the ring on her finger. It was always there. "Davy," she said, "are you sorry for your old granny?"

He nodded, and for the first time he looked into her bright old eyes. But he looked away.

"You're never sick," she said. "You're so full of life."

A fly buzzed onto the bedspread and he looked at it, but he did not flick it away.

"You could help your old granny if you wanted to." She waited. "Did you hear me?"

"Yes," he said. "How?"

But she did not seem to know. She looked away. After all, what she asked was impossible . . .

"Just sit here," she said. "Don't go away." And she tightened her crooked fingers around his arm. She could feel the pulse beating beneath his skin and the need in his blood to be under the cottonwoods.

Like a great dark bird her own need circled waiting to light.

When her son came in for supper she was sitting up in bed with the pillows to her back. He stood in the doorway and stared at her. "You're sitting up," he said at last. Saying it, his voice was a little stupid. It had been months, almost a year, since he had seen her sitting.

She looked away from him with a shyness. "I'm better," she said with a quiver in her voice, almost girlish.

He could not take it in. "But how . . . is it the dry weather, do you think?"

She shook her head, but it did not seem a denial.

"I'm so glad," he said, and indeed, as he thought of it, it was the first time he had felt glad since Mary had died.

Then he asked, "Where's Davy?" And he looked past her bed and through the window.

A little shadow passed over her face. "He seemed tired. I think . . . he's in his room."

"Tired!" said the father, scoffing. "Davy! At this time of day?" But he went away from her down the hall.

Davy lay on his back across the bed. His eyes were open and dark with the dusk at the top of the room. Over him was pulled a blue-and-gray quilt his mother had finished before her death. His father looked down at him.

"Hey, son. What's this?" He spoke with a loving roughness. It troubled him now to see the quilt his wife had made with her living hands. And then, after all, it was summer . . . "Are you cold?" he asked. He sat down abruptly beside the boy and a fleeting pain clouded the small open eyes. Wayne put his hand on the boy's still face. It was cool. He drew aside the quilt, as if he were putting away the hand of his wife. "What's wrong, fella?" Then he saw the still arms and the tiny swelling about the wrists and the joints of the fingers.

He sat and looked at his son for an endless time and he could not think. The black woman Lou came down the hall, stopping outside the door, calling supper. He answered her, but he did not stir. Twilight began to come into the room.

The boy stirred once.

Wayne bent over him. "Do you feel sick?" But the boy shook his head, and in the twilight his eyes were fixed.

And Wayne drew the quilt back over the boy. Then he got to his feet and went down the hall to his mother's room.

She sat in the half-light, relaxed and younger. The way she had looked five years ago when she first came to live with them, before this sickness. But perhaps it was only the flattering twilight.

He switched on the harsh light over her bed. She drew her hand quickly to shade her eyes, not slowly, painfully . . . She did not protest. She only sat there with her hand above her eyes, as if she were looking down a long, sunny road.

"What did you do to him?" he said at last.

It took her a moment to answer. "What do you mean?"

He came into the room and faced her. "He's sick," he said. "His wrists are swelled up. His fingers too." He looked at her own. She had taken off the ring. He could see the dark line where the gold had marked it.

She lowered her hand over her eyes and began to tremble. But he went to her and tore away her hand and looked her full in the face. "Why are you better?" he said. "Tell me that." And he did not sound like her son but like a stranger, like an enemy . . . or like God.

She began to weep piteously. "I didn't do anything. Please, Wayne, I didn't . . . I wouldn't hurt him for anything."

"But you did," he said. "How?"

"Nothing," she wept. "Nothing. I only wanted to get better . . . And he had so much . . . so much . . . life in him."

"What are you talking about?" he asked brutally.

"I thought he could spare a little . . . I told him to sit here. And I touched him and he wanted to help. That was all."

"But what did you do to him?"

"Nothing!" she cried out to the room in despair. "He just sat here for an hour. Maybe longer, I couldn't tell. But I could feel . . . I was getting better."

He stared at her with eyes gone cold and strange. He was thinking: Why didn't you go on and die? Why did it have to be Mary and not you? Why does it have to be Davy and not you?

She could tell his thought. And her mind cried back at him: Wait till you're old. Can I help it if I have to live? Can I help it if I want to be well? Like you and Davy?

He turned on his heel and went back to his son. The smell of food from the kitchen came down the hall and half sickened him.

He lay on the bed beside his son. And the quilt that his wife had made was against him, as if she slept again by his side. His son's quick breathing became her breath. And he wept for them both.

Then he lay with his mind on fire, trying to reason, to understand, knowing he should get up and go for the doctor but sure of the emptiness of the gesture. And the boy beside him neither stirred nor slept, neither lived nor died, but lay as his grandmother had till tonight. Wayne strained his ears for her light, restless cough. But tonight she slept. In the house her sleep lay heavy as incense.

The boy made a sighing sound in his throat. Wayne eased his cumbrous length from the bed. He stood beside it, oppressed with the strangeness of having lain in his work clothes, weak with the bitter taste of the room. Remembering the way it had been in the past. Rising in the winter before it was daylight to go to work. Getting up, leaving his wife asleep. Going to the window, looking out at the darkness, hearing his wife in her sleep move into the warm bed-space he had left, as if she became his sleeping self, as if she became his warm real self. As if all the life they both possessed was heavy and warm on the bed where she lay . . . And then the cold air of the winter room would give him strength and a separate life. When he moved about putting on his clothes, the corners of the room were filled with his life, and his wife lay sleeping and rich with his life. And if she stirred and threatened to wake he paused and breathed deeply, and her own breath lengthened again into sleep. So much life was his own to use and to share . . .

Now he fell on his knees beside the bed. He cried to his child, I'm no good to you, Davy. He cried to himself, I let this happen. I let my life go. I died with her. I let all the life go out of this house. He tried to remember what God was like.

Then he stood up and stumbled away from the room, past his mother's sleep, and into the room where his wife dwelt at night. He began to walk aimlessly through it in darkness, touching the bedpost, the dresser, the closet where her clothes still hung. He cried out to her: I have to go. I have to leave you. I have to live . . . To breathe was pain in his throat and his chest. For dearer, far dearer to him than his life was her living dead presence that he now dismissed.

Then he was out in the hall again. The house was strange. And new in the way it had been before in the time when at night he had dreamed these rooms and then by day had labored to build them. He had known the house then in its very bones. And while it was growing, the child who lay now at the end of the hall was growing too in its mother's bones. And now the room at the front lay in wait. Moonlight rimmed the shades at the windows. He felt for the chair where in the evening she always sat sewing. He touched the lamp on the table beside it. In anguish he dragged the chair from the lamp and placed it firmly against the wall.

Faltering, he crossed the hall to the kitchen where deep in his lungs was the food she had cooked for him. It was always there, even after a year, beneath the smell of the daily meals that the woman fixed and he tried to eat. It was in the walls, in the wood of the shelves. Whispering, weeping, and turning in pain from counter to sink, he pulled down a cloth that Lou had left drying, filled a pan with water, and then he began to wash down the walls with great, sweeping strokes from ceiling to floor. Moving in darkness, he groped with his massive hands for the spaces. Something fell and broke. He went on washing the room in darkness, pressing into the walls till his arms were cramped and the bones of the house were again laid bare. Or so it seemed to him now in his pain.

When he reached the door to the porch, he laid down his cloth and the pan beside it. He opened the screen and went out slowly into the night. His feet were bare, but he could not recall taking off his shoes. He walked uncertainly, feeling beneath him the ragged patches of grass and sand. Beyond him the field lay throbbing with moonlight, as if it were water surrounding his house. He remembered his land was once covered with sea. He was not surprised that tonight it returned. In the shadow of the cottonwoods he stopped and waited. He could hear the whispering high in the branches. He listened intently, wanting the voices, the clamor of leaves, the sound of a small boy's racing feet. He tore a great handful of leaves from above and filled his lungs with their old-new smell of summer and green. Then with infinite purpose he washed himself, scrubbing his face, his arms, and his chest, rubbing the rough leaves into his skin till his flesh was seared and aflame with his blood.

When he was done, he waded slowly into his field, wading deep in the moonlit sea, ancient and warm and pulsing with light. On his face the moon was as warm as the sun. He walked in circles, stumbling, reeling. The soles of his feet were pierced with the stubbles. He lost his way, till he found himself by the wooden fence that surrounded the barn. He clung to it, pulling himself along, catching his clothes on the weathered planks. The splinters of rough oak stabbed his arms. And then he was standing beside the pump where, home from the field in his daylight world, before entering the house he would wash his hands. He fell against it, bracing himself. Slowly at first, he was moving the handle. Its iron wail came from his own dry throat calling the water from deep in the ground. When the burst of it came, he knelt beneath it, drinking it, drenching himself in the flood, now with face upturned, now with his head bowed low to receive it, his mouth alive with its iron taste of the earth and the moon. When the water failed he heard his own voice cry his name to fling and scatter it over the trees, the barn, the field, sowing his shattered name like seed, till it smelled of bitter roots and mold and the night world stopped his breath with loam . . .

He cried for a sign that his life would green.

He grew aware that his horse was nosing him through the fence. He stood up, dripping, to grope for the nose, the eyes, and the mane. The horse moved closer, pressing his flanks to the wooden boards. And the man leaned into him, clutching the broad, warm back and the sides. With the shock of the water the great flanks shuddered and rippled with light, but they did not shrink. The animal waited, loving his touch, sensing his need, listening, waiting. They waited together, drenched in moon, sharing the midday field, the hay, the fresh-ploughed earth where the hooves would stumble and cake with mud, the willow branches that caught in the mane . . . till his hands on the flank were soaked with its life. Till, faltering, he crossed the yard to the house, the house he had built with the life of those hands. He passed them over the warm rough bricks, touching the bricks with his face and lips. At last he entered and walked down the hall past his mother's sleep and his empty room, a weary road, to the bed of his son.

He stood there whispering and calling his name and whispering his own, the name he used to be called as a child. And whispering, he took off his cool wet clothes and lay down naked upon the bed. Gently he pulled the small body over and onto his own, face against face, chest against chest, the small feet dry and cold on his thighs. The boy moaned into him, still awake. He folded the limp arms like broken wings. Over them both he drew the quilt that his wife had made for this holy night. Then he folded the whole of the child in his arms . . .

When he awoke the moon had set. The darkness was dense and harder than stone. The boy in his arms was not moving or breathing . . . The two lay rooted in stony dark. Then slowly he knew that the breath in the body was matching his own, so softly, so perfectly he had thought it his own. The boy slept over him into his flesh.

He passed his hands down the arms he had pinioned, from shoulder to wrist where his own blood sang with the boy's warm pulse, then to fingers, feeling each one in turn. He folded them, slender and firm, in his own.

Starwood

In the middle of the morning he fell asleep while his life was balanced and tipped and spilled. It had been like holding the cup of cream soda she had brought him to drink and drowsing and waking to find it gone. He could not account for falling asleep nor could he recover what sleep had erased. It was vital to recall the waking part exactly as it had come to pass.

The train had slowed, jerked him out of sleep, then spun him along with a clicking of rails. It picked up speed and clattered awhile, then slowed again. He was almost back in the nest of sleep. He heard a man's voice calling, "Starwood." And the train was stopping. Steps were coming, going away. Someone bumped his arm. He was next to the aisle.

Then Tess was speaking against his ear. He remembered the moving soft of her lips. She said in an ordinary voice: "I'm starved . . ." It sounded to him like an echo of "Starwood." Perhaps she had simply repeated the name. But it must have been "starved," for then she exclaimed, "I see a man outside sellin' grapes! Ben, you want a grape?" He shook his head. "People are gettin' off and buyin'. I'll get you one. Ben, I'll be back . . ." And then she had kissed him on the cheek. It was the last he knew of her — the brush of her lips, then the brush of her skirt as she stepped across his outstretched legs.

His mind had surfaced some time later, like a swimmer slowly released from depths. The train was swinging at a comfortable speed. He had opened his eyes and stared ahead. It was when the train went into a tunnel that he was aware in the sudden dusk of the overhead lights that he traveled alone. Tess was afraid of all the tunnels. "It's like a cave," she had said with each and touched his shoulder with the side of her face. Then, without even turning his head, he knew that the seat beside him was empty. Even then he knew in a corner of his mind that it had been empty for quite some time. But at once he stifled the intuition and sat up and stared before and behind. And when his car emerged from the tunnel he felt his disquiet a foolish thing. He sat back and waited for her to return from the rest room just ahead or from a walk the length of the train or from talking to someone in another car. She forgot about time. The train slowed for a stop and braked and waited, squeaking and puffing, while people walked through the car getting on and off. He found he was still a little asleep and the mild commotion came out of a dream. He closed his eyes, then opened them swiftly and stood up and walked the length of the train, and then, in a kind of mounting panic, back again through the cars to the rear.

He found himself stopping strangers and asking, "Have you seen a lady, small, white blouse, dark hair with braids around her head?" They looked at him without any interest and shook their heads in assorted ways. The porter barely paused for him. "They gets on and gets off . . . No, I ain't noticed no one answers that description. Like I say, they gets on and off. They gets so they all looks about the same."

By now the train was moving again. He stood in the rear near the coupling of cars where the sway was greatest. He could feel the lurch in his hands and his throat. The rhythm pounded his fear into shreds. It was on his tongue, metallic and acid. My little wife . . . my little wife . . . Again he searched the cars. They were empty as husks. They were full of people but empty as husks.

He stationed himself between two of the cars, watching the banks and the fences rush past, bracing himself as the metal plates shifted beneath his feet, as the gravity center of his life was shifting. While the distance grew he desperately waited for the train's next stop.

He got off at a place called Broadwater. No taxi around, no train going back until tomorrow. Only a bus that left in two hours. The town seemed deserted. He called the train station back in Starwood. At last there was an answer in a reedy voice. It was the ticket man. "Ain't no one in the waitin' room answers that description. No, I can't see the platform. Not from here I can't . . ." Then a long, breathy whistle. "Hey, Greavy, you see a woman out by the tracks?" He was back again. "We got no one here answers that description." "Take my name. It's Caan." He spelled it out.

While he waited for the bus he called Edith in Atlanta. She took a long time. "Where are you?" she said. "In New Orleans?"

"Edith . . . we're not there. I'm in a place called Broadwater in north Alabama. Have you heard from Tess? Did she call?"

"I don't understand. Why would Tess call?"

He began to explain. He tried to sound calm. "I'm headin' back to Starwood. I'm waitin' on the bus."

"You call me, now. As soon as you know you call me. Hear?"

"I'll call you," he said. And he hung up quickly, beginning to hear the words she was thinking: I always thought she was young for you. You forty-four and her twenty-three. Three years ago she had said them out, but when they were married she wished them all the happiness there was. In the war they had wired that her son was missing. It gave her a look of not believing in happiness . . .

He called Starwood again and the reed voice answered, "She ain't showed up."

Caan was nearly two hours on the bus. It seemed to be stopping at every crossroads, forever slowing and picking up speed. He didn't know why he was sweeping the countryside with his eyes when he knew it was Starwood where she would be. Some trifling thing had kept her from getting back on the train. She could have gone to the rest room and forgot about time. She was bad about time. She would say, "Oh, Ben, is it time to eat? How could it be time! I haven't fixed anything." Sometimes they would eat . . . maybe eight o'clock. He couldn't care less. She would watch him eat like a soft little bird settling down in the dust.

With his jaw locked tight against his fear, he pressed with the palm of his open hand the silver chain he wore on his wrist. She had given it to him the day they were married. It had a small plate with his name engraved. "It's so I can find you in case you're lost." No room on the back for their address, so she'd had the number of their phone engraved. "Then they can call me up and say, 'We found somethin', ma'am, that belongs to you.' And I can say, 'Fine, I'll be right there.' " And he had said, "Are you sure you'll come?" And she had said, "I'm almost there."

He said it now as he rode to her: I'm almost there . . . I'm almost there. Over and over: I'm almost there.

Then a sign read "Starwood," and the bus let him off at the side of the road a block from the station. It was squat and weathered, painted yellow and brown. While the bus roared away he tried to feel hope and a surge of relief. There was only his coldness in the noonday sun and his fear of the station where she might not be. There was no one about. The town appeared to be blocks away.

Carrying his suitcase, he went inside and swept the one empty room with his eyes. The platform beyond it was quite deserted. The ticket man stood and narrowly watched him. He was old and slight, with a shock of white hair that dwarfed his face. In one hand he held a segment of sausage and in the other a soft-drink can. His hands shook gently.

When Caan approached him the man called out in his reedy voice, "She ain't showed up." As if in his mind the voice on the phone and the searching face had touched and sparked.

Caan halted, then seeing the door marked "Women," he walked straight toward it. The ticket man raised his voice at once. "That ain't allowed."

Without hesitation Caan opened the door and looked inside. The room was empty. Water dripped from a faucet with a fretful sound. He swallowed the panic that rose in his throat. "You got a police station somewhere around?"

The old man considered the question in silence. Then he gestured toward the town with a trembling finger. "What kinda woman is that you lost?"

"My wife," said Caan. And at once the two words bound his breath. When he reached the door the man called again: "You been married long?"

Caan did not turn. "Long enough," he said.

On the walk into town he could not think what he had meant by the words. They seemed to strike against the knot of his fear. It was good to be moving, but soon he was there. Two blocks of stores and a buckling sidewalk. And everything jammed, as if all had been whirled and thrown to the center. Then the town thinned to nothing in every direction. Sandlots sprouted grass. A junkyard rusted with pickups bedded in jimson weed. In the distance lay a school where the patchy asphalt turned to gravel. There seemed to be no people about. It was noon and perhaps they were home for lunch. "Closed" signs were on several of the windows and screens. In every doorway he looked for Tess.

He lost the sidewalk and turned to the right, and again he lost it, till at last beside him was a small building front with "Police Station" lettered in black on the glass. He went inside. A rich scent of creosote hung in the air. At his feet was a whimpering long-haired setter. There were green file cabinets, and on top of one of them a basket of figs.

An officer in khaki, his sleeves rolled up, came in from the rear, eyed Caan with suspicion, and put the figs in a drawer of the cabinet. "What's yer business? Shut up," he said to the dog on the floor.

The dog moaned once.

Caan schooled his voice. "It's my wife. She got off the train here and never got back on."

Middle-aged and heavy, the man looked through the window and back to Caan. In their cradles of flesh his eyes were round and copper as coins. He was chewing something. The folds of his cheeks were rising and falling. "You sayin' she's in Starwood?"

"She's got to be."

The man rubbed the back of his neck, still chewing. "How long she been missin'?"

"Since around ten o'clock."

"Ten o'clock today?" He looked at the clock on the station wall. "Well, now, that ain't long. Officially . . . legally . . . nobody ain' missin' in that length a time. Where yer from?"

"We were travelin' from Nashville to New Orleans."

The phone rang on his desk, and the man turned to get it. Caan saw a square bandage taped to his head. While he talked about fishing his flat, official voice took on genial warmth, and he stroked his pad of gauze with a loving hand. Caan watched his gesture and rocked his own need in the pit of his chest till he wanted to cry out at the forced delay. The fumes from the creosote smarted his eyes.

The officer hung up and turned to Caan. He rolled down his sleeves and buttoned them slowly.

"She's here," said Caan. "She got off to buy grapes. She never got back on."

The officer hooted. "That's a new one," he said. "Ain' nobody aroun' here sellin' grapes in the station."

A young man dressed in khaki came in through the back. "Titus . . . you ever seen someone sellin' grapes in the station?"

The young man stopped. His face was freckled. His hair was brick red, with sideburns bleached a mottled yellow and white. "What kinda grapes, sir?"

"Any kinda grapes."

The boy shook his head. The officer asked, "What was you doin' all the time this went on?"

"I went back to sleep. I thought she'd get back on."

The officer laughed and rubbed his jaw. "Seems like you don' look after yer wife none too good."

Despair and resentment took away Caan's breath. He asked it humbly, "Will you help me find her?"

"Well, hold on a minute. Let me git this straight. You was on this train but you ain' on it now. Where yer comin' from?"

"I got off at Broadwater. I took the bus here."

The officer picked up a file from the desk and walked to a cabinet and put it inside. Caan could see the figs before he shut the drawer. The boy was watching with rapt attention. The man glanced at the clock. "She ain' missin' till noon t'morrer."

"You got a hotel here?" Caan finally said. "Someplace I could stay?"

"Well, now, we got a motor court edge a town." When Caan did not move he studied him briefly. "I can give you a figger an' this is a fact: ninety-five percent shows up by the followin' day. Ain't that a fact, Titus?"

"Yes, sir, they shows up or the body gits found."

"Titus," said the officer, "you gotta lot lef' to learn. You never mention a body till you got one to show. You got that, boy?"

"Yes, sir, I got it."

Caan picked up his suitcase and went back out. There were tears in his eyes from the creosote fumes and the bright noon sun and a kind of bewilderment shafting his heart. There were birds overhead. He could hear their cries, fold upon fold of them cleaving the sky. He walked beneath them back to the train station with a failing hope she would be there at last. His suitcase seemed to be filled with stones. As he crossed the waiting room on his way to the platform, the ticket man followed him with wary eyes.

Caan sat on the bench with the suitcase before him. A small wind was moving the shred of a ticket to the edge of the track. After a while Caan looked up to see the slight form in the doorway.

"You gotta buy a ticket 'fore you git on the train. I reckon you know that."

"I'm not leavin'," Caan said.

The man waited, swinging his foot in the sun. He smelled of pickle. "You ain't give up, I see."

Caan did not reply. The ticket man walked to the edge of the platform to spit in the weeds. He swayed a little, like a bird ill at ease on a moving branch. His white hair ruffled and bloomed in the air. He looked at the sky. "Gon' rain," he said and returned to his counter.

Caan sat without moving. The track before him ran away into sunlight. A hound dog crossed it and disappeared into moving pines. A lone buzzard circled the brush beyond. A swarm of blackbirds whirled against the rails like jet beads scattered by a hand in the sky. Then while he watched them the brightness clouded. The rails went gray on the coral earth, and the birds flew away into leaden sky. His foot touched the suitcase he and Tess had packed. They had only one that would do them proud. Her things on the right side and his on the left. He could see in his mind's eye the things she had taken. She had asked his opinion about each one. Now he sat in the grayness and thought of last night before they had left as if it belonged to their pattern of nights. From the day they were married a part of him never fell into sleep but lived for them both in the singing dark. It seemed to him now they had never left home. They were waiting for dawn. While she slept he was living their secret life and keeping it safe until they awoke . . .

The wind was stirring. The pines across the tracks began to rouse. And then it was raining with a clatter of drops on the platform roof. Lightning sprang from the clouds and into the pines.

The ticket man called aloud from the door. "Ain't allowed to sit out there in a storm."

Caan turned around. Mirrored in the glass were lashing pines. There were smoking clouds gone dark as if it were night in the glass. He could see Tess walking alone in the rain.

"Man got struck by lightnin', reckon five year ago."

It was blowing rain now. Caan could feel the wet on his face and his hands. Then thunder broke, and out of its crash came the roar of the train. The platform shuddered. He could see the faces looking out at him as they whizzed away. He searched them all with a passionate gaze. Through the windows beyond them a vision of pines was hazed and distorted.

The wind and rain roared past like the train. Caan could not think. After a while he went inside. He had seen a telephone booth in the corner. He dialed Edith again. "You got any word?"

"No, I haven't, Ben. Ben, what do you think?"

"I don't know," he said. "But I'm stayin' here. There's a motor court somewhere around they say. You can reach me there if you hear anything . . . The best you can do is stay with the phone."

He went back to the bench and sat there watching the swaying trees, dispossessed, drifting into dream, remembering how they had met at the fair. He had bulls to show and a white-faced heifer, which won a ribbon. She stood there stroking the head of the heifer with tears in her eyes. Seeing him approach, she called, "Is this yours?" And when he nodded, "She's afraid," she said. "Can't you tell she's afraid?" She placed her small hand on the throat of the heifer. And then she looked up at the arching roof of the coliseum. "It's like a cave in here. It makes her afraid." And indeed when he touched her the heifer was trembling, so slightly he had not noticed before. "Take her home," she said. "Please take her home." "I will," he promised, "as soon as I can." She offered at once, "I'll stay with her till you're ready to go."

He came back later to find her kneeling in the trampled dirt with her hands on the rail of the small enclosure and her face to the head of the white-faced heifer. They were locked in stillness. He had loved her then. He had never really cared for a woman before. Not wholly, like this, without thought or reason. He gave her the jar of his sourwood honey (blue ribbon and all). It was the color of her eyes. Then, because she seemed quite alone, he took her home in his truck, with the animals standing like sheaves in the rear. She was visiting the mother of a friend she said. She had a job back in Lexington.

After they were married he asked her what kind of job it was. "I forget," she said. "It was so long ago. Before you came I was lost in a cave. You found me, Ben."

"You worked in a cave?"

But she only laughed. When he asked her things she would pick up the little banjo she had brought and play something sad and dance to the tune. Not really dance but move like a shadow, dipping and turning. He didn't know that a banjo could sound like that, like a tiny harp, the way she made it sound. She plucked the loneliness out of the strings and wove it into the floor with her feet. "I love you, Tess . . . I love you, Ben." She would sing his words and then her own and dance them into the room with her feet.

He became aware of the rain on his face. He was suddenly appalled that her clothes in the suitcase could be getting wet. He stood up quickly and took it inside.

"You ain't give up?" said the ticket man. He was smoking a pinch of a cigarette, which jabbed away at the empty air.

"Ain't allowed to give up," Caan said to him gravely. He walked through the door and into the rain. Then his eyes were cutting across the fields, pausing at torpid shapes of green, scanning the doorways, searching for shadows in dormer windows, till his vision blurred in the drifting rain.

There were two small beds, one against each wall, and a smell of pine cleaner. He opened the suitcase to find dry clothes and there were hers. He plunged his hand into them, held it there, then withdrew it slowly and shut the lid.

He lay on the bed with its chocolate spread. The ceiling was patterned with water stains. He recalled her voice in the moving train, the brush of her lips, the brush of her skirt. And then he recalled how it was he awoke but with eyes still closed, how everything seemed to unfold in his waking. He had not remembered it all till now: the liquid sense of crossing water, then the brightness that flowered beyond his lids with the open field, then the shadow of forest, then water, then fields, then the tunnel, the dusk, the lights overhead, and his mounting awareness that he was alone . . .

He would hold in the sunlight her sweet, still face. "How come you want to marry an old man like me?"

"Ben, you're not old."

"When I see you I'm not."

"How come you want to marry a dumb thing like me? Never been anywhere. Never done anything."

"I been enough places for both of us," he said.

"Don't cook too good."

"I ate enough food to last me my life."

"Don't sew too good."

"Got all my buttons sewed on tight."

They used to go on in this smiling way. Like singing it was, making love this way. Even after their marriage they talked like this and all of it true. She couldn't do anything all that well. But the words she could say were so simple and soft they seemed to settle on him like doves. Or they sang to him like a thrush in the wood.

"Ben, how come you didn't get married before?"

"I was waitin' for a woman never been anyplace. Couldn't cook or sew."

She had always wanted to go somewhere. When he told her they would take a trip to New Orleans, she clapped her hands. "Now I can say that I been someplace." When his mail would come, like a child she would look at all the postmarks. "Ben, this is from Knoxville. Look, this is New York." She never got any mail, so he handed her half of his to open, the ones with the postmarks farthest away, making a game of it, catching her smile . . .

He turned on the bed. The chocolate spread had an odor of coffee.

Before they left a card had come for her from Phoenix, Arizona, forwarded from Lexington, where she had lived. He brought it from the mailbox and read it on the way. It was from someone named Joan, and it said: "I got to thinking about all the fun last time you were here. Why don't you come out unless you got a job or got married or something. I gave your address to Sam. Hope it's o.k."

She took it and read it. "This isn't for me. I never knew any Joan." Or Sam? he thought. "Or Sam," she said. "Should I save the stamp? I think it's still good . . . It's crazy," she said. "You reckon there's a Tess Hamill somewhere else?"

"Just one," he said. "Couldn't be another."

The room grew dark. It was raining still, with a clamorous sobbing of water and leaves. He fell into sleep. For a while he seemed to be waiting alone on the platform bench. And then in the rain he lay with her, holding and folding her, dreaming her there.

He awakened early. The rain was gone. He walked in the sun back into the town. There were holes in the street full of water and leaves. There were voices and motors, a wagon or two, and faces of strangers that stared at him. He was in the police court promptly at ten. The officer looked up from his desk by the wall. A sign on white cardboard gave his name as Bailey. Caan was sure that it had not been there before. Bailey stared at him, then swept his eyes to the clock on the wall. "I figgered she'd show at the court."

"How would she show up? She doesn't know I'm here."

"Well, now, I tol' you she ain' officially missin' till noon."

"She got off here about ten o'clock."

" 'Bout ten, you say . . . It seems to me if it was my wife I'd know close to certain when she got off the train."

Caan resisted the anger. A truck outside shifted gears and roared. He asked it humbly as he had before: "Will you help me find her?"

Bailey waited, caressing the patch on his head. "Now, what I can do, I can call the sheriff. And then I can call the state troopers. If she's wandering somewheres down the road they might could spot her. And if she's somewheres back in the woods the sheriff has got hisself a posse. If he's willin' to use it. I can't guarantee what the sheriff'll do. Sometimes he don't take too well to things. 'Specially if he's got a mind to go huntin' . . . If it comes to bloodhounds, you willin' to pay?"

"Yes, I am."

"If it comes to them, can you come up with somethin' belongs to yer wife?"

Caan nodded, for a moment unable to speak. "But what about here? What if she's somewhere close around here?"

Bailey tipped his chair back into the wall. "I guess I'm gonna have to explain it to you. You may not've noticed but Starwood ain't exactly a city. And just about all they can pay for is me. And I can't leave here and let the town go to hell. I got me a deputy three days a week. But he ain' very big as you may a noticed and he don't know much, but he's fulla idears." Bailey chuckled a moment. "But he ain' on duty. Comes in t'morrer. Now, the best thing to do is give me a reel good description of yer wife and I'll pass it on."

Caan waited all day for the call to come that could free him at last or lock him forever into his loss. He sat in a corner of the station by the window, watching the street as if she might appear. As if she might find him. "I lost you, Ben."

Once through the window for a shattering moment he thought he saw her. A woman approached him across the street, then her image dissolved into that of a stranger. He saw her pass with tears in her eyes.

Bailey smoked incessantly from a stub of cigar. The narrow room slowly filled with a haze, which lay with the phantom odor of creosote. Caan could not believe in the worth of their efforts: the endless wait for the sheriff to ring and Bailey's occasional call to the troopers to talk with a woman he seemed to know well. Twice Bailey advised him to wait at the motor court. Caan shook his head. His body, gone tense, could scarcely move. But his mind was hovering above the roads, wandering through lanes he had only glimpsed, scanning the doorways, searching the windows, stalking shadows that thinned into mist.

A boy came in who had lost his dog. A woman had been bitten by a dog next door. She wanted a warrant to comfort her pain.

At five o'clock Bailey rose to announce: "Gotta close up here. After five the station moves to my house." He sounded relieved.

"But they know I'm there. If anythang comes in I know where to reach you." In the street he looked Caan full in the face. "I don't think yer wife is aroun' here, Caan."

When Caan opened the door to his room, for one moment of joy he thought that Tess had returned. Then he saw it was Edith who sat in the chair. And the fact of her presence sealed the fact of his loss.

She rose to kiss him and read his face. "I'm sorry, Ben . . . I had to talk the manager into lettin' me in. Lucky for me, I had a snapshot of us all together tucked in my wallet."

By an effort of will he kept from breaking. "Do you know anything?"

She shook her head.

He lay down at once on the bed by the window.

"Ben, I had to come." His eyes were closed. "When you were little, after Mama died, it was like she told me to look after you . . . When you had bad dreams I would sleep with you. You remember that?"

She stood over him then. But he would not take his arm from his face. "Ben, talk to me."

"There's nothin' to say. She's gone. That's all."

"Are they tryin' to find her?"

"They call it that."

Then he looked at her worn, slightly puffed and florid face. She was older than he by a good six years. The lines rayed out from her pale blue eyes that always seemed on the brink of tears. In one of them she was nearly blind. It was clouded a bit, like the agate marble he had lost as a child. She was stronger than he. He had always known it.

"Are you glad to see me?"

"I said I wanted you to stay by the phone."

"I know," she said, "but I had to come."

He closed his eyes. He listened to a fly beat into the screen. "I'm glad you're here." Without saying a word they waited in light that was turning gray. "How did you get here?" he finally asked.

"I brought the car. Hicks can get a ride."

She went out finally to find some food. He tried to eat a little to please her. "I keep thinkin' that I'm really asleep."

She sat on the bed against the wall. She kept her watery eyes upon him. He could see them glisten from across the room. Her voice was toneless and groping for words. "She always seemed . . . unsettled to me. To me she did. One minute high up and talkin' a blue streak. And the next . . . Of course a sweet little thing."

"What are you sayin'?"

"I'm not sayin' a thing."

The smell of food was filling his throat.

"What about her clothes? Did she have a suitcase?"

"We packed together." He gestured toward the opened bag on the floor.

"Did she have anything else? Like another little bag?"

"What are you sayin'?"

"I'm just askin', Ben."

He lay still, thinking. And suddenly he saw it, the long little bag with the leather strap. He was amazed that he had not recalled it before. "Yes, she did," he said. "I forgot about it. A kind of a narrow little bag. She said she wanted to bring it along."

"Where is it?" she asked.

He stared at the ceiling. "I don't know," he said.

"Was it left on the train?"

"I don't know," he said.

She waited a little. "Was it big enough for a change of clothes?"

"What are you sayin'?"

"I'm not sayin' a thing. But Ben, we got to talk it out."

"I'm tired of talk."

"Then sleep," she said. "I can tell you need it more than anything."

He was thinking of the rain the night before and the sound of the wind, how it sucked and sighed . . . "I could miss the phone."

"I'll listen for the phone. That's why I'm here."

He laughed a little. "I was wonderin' why." He seemed to be laughing inside a sleep. The tension began to go out of his throat and then his chest. The rest of his body he could not feel.

"God," she said, "this place is quiet . . . It's funny. I never heard of this town." She kicked off her shoes. He heard them strike the floor and the whimper of springs as she stretched on the bed. A car door slammed. People were moving into the court. He could hear the anger and then the laughter.

"What about her relatives? Will you let them know?"

He roused a little. "She hasn't got any, Edith. She came from an orphanage."

"You never told me that . . . But there must be somebody. Even with orphans there's usually someone. Who put her there?"

"She doesn't know." After a while he found he could say it. "She told me this. Someone left her inside a cave."

She watched him in wonder. "How do you mean, Ben?"

"She said she was found when she was several weeks old wrapped up in blankets near the mouth of a cave. Inside the opening against the wall. She said she was told that. It was one of those caves that you pay to go in. Somebody paid for the tour and left her. Somebody thought it had been a man."

She sat up straight in bed. "Ben, do you really think that could be right?"

"I don't know. It's what she said. I think she believed it."

She lay back down. "Ben, that's strange."

After a while he went on with the rest. "When she got older she had a thing about caves. She said she wanted to be around them. Not go inside. She might get left again. But stand around and watch people come out. She thought she might see the one that left her comin' out."

"After all those years?" He did not answer. "But if he left her when she was a baby . . . how would she know him?"

"She said she dreamed what his face was like." He heard the far-off sound of the train like an infant crying alone in the dark. "She thought he might go back to a cave because he was sorry for what he'd done."

"Oh, Ben!"

He lay still thinking how after they were married she had said, "Ben, I married you because you look like him."

"Ben, she's lived in a dream."

"I know it," he said. "But I was in her dream."

Then they both lay still with the room between them. He heard the train coming close and closer. "It's the train," he said. Then it seemed to carry them both into night. He heard her breathing and knew that she slept. But he went on speaking. And now he was freed

by the sound of her sleep to speak of his wife with burning whole-
ness, of their love in the twilight, of how he unwound the shining circle of her braided hair, unraveled it slowly, and caught it lightly between his lips, then shook it like rain on his face and throat. Of how
he would kiss the scar that lay along her arm like a coral chain to
adorn her flesh. She could never recall how it came to be. "It was
always there." It was there for him. Of how he would watch her in the
light of dawn. She lay drowned in sleep till his eyes called her up to
the world of day and she woke to his love . . . she woke to his love.

Now he kissed, not the coral chain of her scar, but the silver chain
she had placed on his wrist . . . so he could be found in case he was
lost.

"I'm lost," he said. In the midst of his speaking he fell asleep. And
finally he dreamt that Tess was calling, "Ben, I'm here." And her
voice was beating the room with echoes that woke him at last to the
morning gray.

Edith was making them cups of coffee with a little electric thing
she had brought. She looked as if she had hardly slept. Her face was
pale and puffed and weary. The agate eye was misted with cloud. In
the early light, as never before, it was clear to him how good she was,
how she wanted to give herself away, to spend herself like a child
with money, to use herself up till she was gone.

"What will you do today?" she asked.

He sat up at once. He saw that her suitcase was by the door. "I'll
look for her." And then he added, "For the rest of my life. If it takes
that long."

Over the rim of her cup she watched him. "You can't look through
the whole world, Ben. Any more than I could with Joey. You got to
do the only, the reasonable thing."

He turned on her fiercely. "You talk like she's some kinda thing I
lost. Like a watch or a dog."

"Look in Starwood," she said. "Then let it be." He listened to
shouts in the court outside. "She got off here. She'll come back to
here. If she can. If she will. Or if she can't she knows how to call you
up at home or how to call me up in Atlanta."

He caught at it quickly. "Yes, she could do that. You better go
back. She could be there now."

"I could settle that." She picked up his phone and dialed and waited. "Hicks, is Tess there? Ben's wife. Is she there?" She was raising her voice. Hicks was hard of hearing. "Did she call? I'll be back today. I'll call. I'll call."

She turned to him then. "There's somethin' I'll say before I go. You haven't got there yet. You got a long way to go before you come to it. But I'm sayin' it now 'cause I won't be around when you need to hear it." She wiped her eyes. "I been there with Joey . . . You make up your mind that it's got to be. And then you decide on the way . . ." He was staring at the bed she had carefully made. He could hear the sound of a truck outside. "The way it was."

He did not move or look at her.

"You decide the way you can live with it best. Then you hold to that. You stick with it, Ben."

He looked at her hard. "What you tryin' to say to me, Edith?"

She wiped her eyes again. "I'm tryin' to tell you that I couldn't bear Joey dyin' some violent way. I didn't want blood or any pain. Or torture. I couldn't live with that. I thought of all the ways it could be. And I took the way I could live with best. And that's the way he went . . . that's the way he went."

He stared at her, not believing her words.

"I can see him lost in the woods, cut off from the rest. And nothin' to eat and gettin' weaker and out of his head with some kinda fever and finally droppin' beside a stream. Trees and birds. A gradual thing. I see his hand in the runnin' water. I see him thirsty and drinkin' the water. I see him sleepin' and never wakin'."

Her face was remote with a kind of peace. But the loss in her words he could not bear.

She waited a little. "Just now when I called . . . I called for Tess, but the way it was I would've been callin' for Joey too. Hopin' against hope a word had come while I was away. Home meant to me the place where the word would come. Whenever I left, I left the place where the word would come. And when I went back, I was goin' back to the place it would come. Home has got to be more."

She walked to the bathroom with her cup and washed it. People outside were loading to leave. A woman said shrilly, "Look at this mess. You expect me to clean up this mess you made?" A car door slammed.

Edith came back and sat on the bed. "Mabel Graham said to me, 'Edith, there's a boy back from there with the woman next door. He might know somethin'. It wouldn't hurt to talk.' 'No, thanks,' I said. I'm glad I can say it. I can say it, Ben, 'cause I got it settled."

She looked at him deeply and then away. "The people I know, they do the same kinda thing with anything hard they got to get past. It's the best way, Ben. Remember I told you."

She stood up slowly. She bent to straighten the chocolate spread. "I'm leavin' you this thing to make coffee with." She walked to the door. "Remember I told you. And when you find it don't tell anyone. You hold it close. I never told Hicks. People can take it away from you, Ben. Just with a look they can take it away."

She went back and kissed the top of his head. "You call me, you hear?"

He took her hands. He had set his mind against her words.

"Ben, it's hard to face things the way they are. Or face not knowin' the way they are. You pick out a way and you stick with it." She turned away. "I said enough. Now I got to go."

He took her suitcase out to the car.

In the station Bailey looked up with a smile. "You say yer wife is younger than you. You git along reel good with yer wife?"

"Yes, I do," said Caan.

"You ever git jealous?"

He steadied his voice. "No, I don't," he said.

"You ever struck yer wife?"

Caan fought his despair. "No, I haven't struck her."

"Well, we gotta look ever thang square in the face."

Caan's voice rose with anger. "I'm sick of talk."

"Caan . . . there is no way, no way I can turn up yer wife if she ain' aroun'. I'm a cop. I ain' some kinda magician."

"But you haven't looked here."

Bailey leaned into the wall with his chair. "Well, Caan, I'll tell you what I can do. This deputy of mine took a course by mail. He likes to practice bein' a bloodhound. And when we ain' busy I take off his leash." He glanced at the clock. "He's due back in ten minutes."

Bailey turned to his desk. When Titus walked in he called him Dick Tracy. "I got you a case here right up yer alley. You got most a the day. But check in again aroun' four o'clock."

The boy's face lit up. His brick-red hair stood up from his head. He stood without moving. "I gotta have Estes."

Bailey looked annoyed. He rubbed his forehead. "After two hours he's on yore payroll."

Outside, they walked through the center of town. Titus reassured Caan. "I'm good with this. Had a lotta experience. I found seven kids different times. No, wait, it was eight. And one ol' man. I'm good with findin' any kinda folks. The thing I do is git into their minds."

He stopped on a curb, and they waited for a light. "Now, is there somethin' more you ain't already tol' about yer wife? I need to git in her mind kinda like."

Caan looked down at the boy, shoulder-high to himself. He could not be more than nineteen at the most, and small for his age. "I've told it. Brown hair. Braid around her head. And small. Real small." It was hard to speak of her in this way.

"That's good," said Titus. "But it ain't helpin' me git into her mind."

They walked to the station, where Titus got the feel of the situation. Then he walked the length of the platform and back. "Whereabouts," he said, "would these grapes be you think? Nobody aroun' here seen anyone with grapes."

"I had my eyes shut. I was half-asleep. I think I said that."

"Did she have a special likin' fer grapes, do you know?"

"I don't know. I don't think so. She was hungry she said."

"I'm tryin' to git in her mind," said Titus.

Caan wanted to turn and walk away. At the same time he dreaded being left with the search. He was beginning to feel a baffled dependence upon the boy.

Titus motioned him to sit on the wooden bench. It was painted rust and covered with leaves. The sun was in Caan's eyes. Titus stood before him with one foot on the bench. "I got to explain the way my mind is workin'. You ever wondered why this town is called Star-

wood? You prob'ly never thought 'less you lived aroun' here. It's got
five roads leadin' out. Like a star, see, has got five different points.
Now, unless yer wife got back on the train while you uz asleep and
got back off again someplace else . . . in which case I don' have no
jurisdiction . . ."

"She wouldn't do that," said Caan.

"Well, providin' she didn't, she'd be aroun' here. And since she
ain't in the station and she ain't in the town . . ."

"How can you know she's not in the town?"

"If she uz in this town we ud know about it. A strange woman in
town is about as outstandin' as a roller coaster slap in the square." He
turned to spit on the concrete behind him. He smoothed his sideburns with the knuckle of a finger. A wind had risen and leaves from
a sycamore were scudding across the platform and into the tracks.
"Now, what my course a action would be is this. I'm sayin' we should
take all five different roads and see what turns up. It's the only pro-
fessional course a action."

It was all a game to the boy, he could see. He closed his eyes to the
sun. He could feel himself back in the moving train, tracing the
length of it, searching the faces and the voices he met. He seemed to
be waiting for her to come, to come out of the station and walk
toward him with her dark hair shining, the braid of it loose and
bright in the sun.

He opened his eyes and looked at the boy. "I want to find my wife.
You understand that, boy?" He said it roughly without meaning the
roughness, but full of the need to say it steady and whole and sure.

Titus nodded twice. "I know that, sir. I'm tryin' to help you."

"Good . . . good. I thank you." He held out his hand and Titus
took it. "I'm beholden to you."

Then he rose with a kind of thirst for the hunt and gave himself
into the keeping of Titus. The boy walked slightly ahead and he followed. They went through the square. There were people standing in
the doors of shops. All of them seemed to be looking at him as if they
had all been told of his plight. Titus ignored them, but greeted with
dignity the few they encountered. Once out of the square Titus
turned to him. "This street we're on turns into a road. It's prob'ly the
likeliest road she'd take, providin' she wanted to take a road."

They walked together at a steady pace. The fields were mowed and tanned with the stubble. The air was dry with a feel of autumn. Trees in the hedges were beginning to turn. Caan could not think why they walked the road. "I don't see a point in this," he said.

"Sir," said Titus firmly, "about yer wife. You see any point in her not gittin' back on the train?" His hair in the sunlight was banner red. "There's a lotta points in this case is strange. I ain't never had a case like it before, which gives me the reason to try ever thang could possibly be. You follow me, sir?"

Caan stared ahead down the red dirt road. "Let's go," he said, "and get it over with."

They walked for a while. There were trees beside them and goldenrod and patches of horseweed white with bloom. They came to a house, unpainted and weathering, back from the road, and Titus said, "Wait here, sir. I need my assistant. It won't take long." He sprinted toward the house.

Caan watched him circle it and disappear. He was dreaming surely. He walked in a dream. He stood in a dream and waited for Titus. He heard dogs barking and a shouted command. It silenced all but a lyric whine that came to him like a snatch of song. Then Titus was back with a black boy hardly half his size wearing overalls and a checkered shirt. His feet were bare. Titus introduced him gravely to Caan. "This is Estes. I sometimes use him as my assistant. When he ain't drunk."

The boy grinned and twisted his feet in the grass. He had a broken tooth near the front of his mouth. He took from behind him a slab of cornbread and began to eat it as they moved along. The crumbs were drifting into the ruts.

Caan walked beside them with mounting despair. The search was slipping from his control. It was turning into a grim charade that children acted for their own delight. He was filled with remorse. Tess was somewhere calling to him, her voice even now was growing faint, and he found himself without power to turn. The road was narrowed as they passed through woods. He could smell the ferns in the shade of trees. Crickets in the ditches whirred and choked and sputtered.

Then they emerged into open meadow. The road became little more than a lane, spongy and slick from the recent rain. Ahead was a giant chestnut oak that towered above all else in the field. Titus pointed to it and left the lane.

Caan stopped and waited.

Titus said, "Estes, shinny up that tree and have a look around."

Estes studied the tree for a bit and whistled. Then he tackled the trunk as if he would throw it and dug in his toes and made the first branch and then the next, and after that he was deep in the green, storming the limbs, bouncing them high, and calling down, his voice muffled with leaves, "What I lookin' fo'?"

Titus spat in the grass. "Anything looks like a woman. Walkin', standin', sittin', or layin' down."

Caan dropped to the grass and covered his face. He had eaten little and was faint with hunger, half-sick with thirst. He was full of anger and then of shame. And then of alarm because he had let slip the whole of a morning that might be crucial, that might be all that was given to him. He could find no logic in what he was doing or in anything done since he left the train. The logic was only that Tess was gone. She had stitched up his life, though she couldn't sew, and now her going had ripped it apart. Her loss was too deep a thing for his tears. But here in the sun it struck him fully. He had held it at bay, but now it fell like the stroke of noon, and the rest of his life was late in the day. He sat with thirst in his afternoon.

"Sir!" said Titus. "Are you o.k., sir?"

He lifted his head to see the boys staring down at him. Swaying a little, he got to his feet.

"Sir," said Titus, "Estes here had a good look around and reports to me he couldn't see a woman of any description."

"I want to go back to town," Caan said.

"I was just about to suggest that, sir. Anyplace else you start from town. There is four other roads as I tol' you, sir."

"Titus," said Caan, "I'm beholden to you. But there won't be any more of this. My wife would have no reason to be wanderin' around the countryside. She's never been here before."

"You sure a that, sir?"

"Of course I'm sure." He was suddenly angry. Unaccountably, the postal from Phoenix flashed into his mind. Estes was pitching rocks at the oak.

Titus lowered his voice. In the sun his cheeks were coppered with freckles. "Sir, I ain't wanted to bring this up, but she coulda been carried. Coulda been foul play."

The fear that had lain on the floor of Caan's mind leapt suddenly upward. He turned away quickly lest his surge of terror find release in wrath and he strike the boy. Without a word he began to stride back toward the town.

Titus ran to keep pace. "If you want my advice . . ."

Caan stopped and faced him. "I don't want your advice. Leave me be. Go back to the station."

The boy flushed deeply under the copper. Caan saw how much he offended him.

Titus turned away. He said in a choked voice: "You need me, sir. I'm the onliest one around is the least bit interested in findin' yer wife." Then he half ran across the field and disappeared in a clump of pines.

Caan watched him go with the aching knowledge that Titus spoke the truth. He walked on, blind to the scene around him. He was conscious finally that a bird was following. But the bird was a whistle, staccato and breathless, as the black boy ran to overtake him.

"Hey! Hey! Hey, mistah!" He was running along beside Caan now, kicking up red dust. "Hey, mistah, I got a granny makes peoples 'member t'ings. You don' b'lieve me? You don' b'lieve me? She make you 'member ever' t'ing . . . ever' t'ing done happen. Even when you's 'sleep.

"C'mon, mistah." He was pleading, coaxing. "She don' charge but a dollah. C'mon, mistah. She don' charge but fifty cents."

Caan turned to him, frowning. "What you talkin' about, kid?"

"Mistah, she cause ol' man Goodson 'member where he lef' his houn' dog when he uz dronk outen his head. She cause Jim Dolan 'member what went wid his money. She cause him 'member who he sittin' nex' to what stole it."

Caan increased his speed, but the boy kept pace. "Hey, mistah, my granny could cause you 'member what went on in dat train rat 'fo' it stop an' what went on while you uz asleep."

Caan heard in a daze how details of his loss had spread like mist through the country roads. He recalled the figures that had stood in the doorways as he left the town. "Leave me be, boy. I got trouble enough."

"Mistah," said Estes, "we is at de rat place. You see dat barn. Yonder hit be . . . My granny live over 'hind dat barn. Jes' de leas' leetle ways. No ways a tall."

Caan stopped and swallowed the stab of his thirst. "How far to town?"

"A good long ways, I b'liged to tell ya . . ." He searched Caan's face. "My granny done got a tree in de yard. You could res' yo'se'f. She got a good swing. You could swing yo'se'f while you studyin' yo' wife an' where she be." Then he said, "Mistah . . . Titus done lef'. Prob'ly won' be back. Hit ain't likely. The onliest one you got lef' is me."

Caan looked at the squirming, dusty form, bent on survival and bent on joy. He smiled a little and rubbed his face. "You think you're a help?"

"Not me, mistah, but my granny she be. She don' charge but a dollah. You needs he'p reel bad."

"I need a drink of water. Your granny got a well?"

"Mistah, she is got de mos' water aroun'. I gonna run on ahead an' start it pumpin' so it be reel cool." He took off running across the field, turning, running backward to see Caan follow, and stumbling, and leaping to catch himself.

Caan waited in the road and then he followed, striding through broomsedge and patches of ragweed where the ground was damp. The house was farther than the boy had insisted. A lethargy born of his thirst and his hunger had broken his spirit, subdued his reason, and he found it impossible to turn aside. He strode with his eyes on the pasture grasses. There was smoke in the air and a glaze on the brown sedge. As far as he could see the creeper grass had ripened like grain and was sweet on the fields with an amber haze.

He looked up and saw the boy ahead, an unpainted cabin, a red dirt yard, and a sycamore tree. Beneath the tree hung a wooden bench of a swing. And around the swing the boy was twirling a small sedge broom, raking the dirt into swirls and circles. He looked up, grinning. "Mistah, I fix you a nice place to set an' study yo' wife while I fetch you de water."

He dropped the broom and ran around the house. Caan looked at the swing and tested its chains. At last he sat down. The boy came running with a pitcher and a Mason jar. The lip of the pitcher was broken off and the water sloshed over his feet when he poured.

"Mistah, I got it reel cool fo' you."

"I'm obliged to you, boy." He drank the water. It tasted of moss and then of iron. It was cold and a long, long time in his throat. He held out the jar and Estes filled it again to the rim, splashing the water on the dirt between them. Caan drank again. He was drinking for Tess. Then he rested his head against the chain of the swing.

"By an' by my granny gonna bring you a biscuit. She got a biscuit save an' stuck in de stove. I tol' her I speck you uz mighty hongry." Under his armpits the blue checkered shirt was bunched and torn.

As if he called her up she was suddenly there, a tall black woman with a yellowish skin and graying hair braided tight and pinned in coils to each side of her head. Her face was small, and beneath white brows her eyes were heavy-lidded and brown as acorns.

"Dis here my granny. Her name is Queen."

She stood very still in her long-sleeved dress and her apron that covered her chest and skirt. She carried a pail and a large tin cup. She studied Caan before she spoke. "I been hearin' 'bout yo' troubles, Mistah Caan. Ever body in dis whole wide worl' got troubles. I he'ps when I can."

"I came for water. I'm obliged to you." He wanted to go but he did not rise.

She skimmed his head with her acorn eyes. "You come fo' he'p. Dat's de size of it. Black or white, dey's all got troubles. Make no diff'rence, I he'ps 'em all."

Then she put the pail on the ground at her feet. "Queen is he'p mo' peoples than she can count. She cain' hardly 'member what all she done. But them folkses 'members. Dey 'members t'ings dat uz lyin' down deep in deir minds an' cain' come up till Queenie he'p."

She looked at a space beside his head. "You want Queen he'p you 'member what happen on dat train rat 'fo' it stop an' 'fo' dat too fo' a good lil spell. Queen can he'p you see to de rat an' de lef'. Queen can he'p you see what behin' yo' head."

Her voice was smooth and flat and dry, as if the words came from her thin, straight lips. But he heard the echo of them in her throat. He was weary and wanted to stay in the swing. She seemed to know. She nodded her head. "Res' yo'se'f a mite. Wouldn't hurt to let yo'se'f swing a mite."

He wanted to go but he made no move. "I got work to do. I got no time for this." He fumbled for coins.

She stared him down. "You gotta fin' yo' wife. Queen gon' he'p. She done tol' you dat." Then she stooped and poured a dark yellow brew from the pail to the cup. It was almost the color of her own tight skin. She circled the cup with her strong old hands. The cords of her hands were binding the cup. Her eyelids closed and her straight lips moved. Then she straightened and handed him the cup to drink. It smelled of leaves.

He drew back at once and set the swing to rocking. Then Estes was down on his knees with the pail. He drank from it deeply. "Look here, mistah. I drinkin' de tea. It don' hurt you none."

Caan wiped his face with his sleeve. There was haze on the field. It seemed to him smoke. It was in his eyes. His weariness mounted and passed into anger. "Understand me, woman. I don't want this craziness. I want my wife." And suddenly his anger was supplication. He reached for the cup and closed his eyes. He was taking the cup from Tess on the train. He drank a little of the yellow brew. It was warm in his mouth and dark and alive. And then in his throat it was dark and dead. He knew he had done an incredible thing.

"Drink a lil mo'. Jes' a lil fo' Queen." Her voice ran as liquid now as the tea.

He swallowed again. He drank of his wife, so close she was. He drank her sweetness and the brown of her hands.

She took the cup. "Now set back an' res' jes' a bit fo' Queen."

He felt a warmth steal across his face. He felt he was rocking on the porch at home. It was only the swing. And Queen was crooning: "You is travelin' away, 'way back in de past. But you comin' back, you packin' yo' grip an' you boardin' de train. You is listenin' to de whistle. You is feelin' de rails. You is travelin' south . . . Now, tell Queen where yo' wife is settin'. Is she settin' to de rat? Is she settin' to de lef'?"

He rocked in the swing. She reached out and took the chain in her hand and stopped its motion. "You tell Queen now. We gotta know dis."

He looked at the ground and the swirls the broom had made in the dirt. "She is on my right. She is by the window."

She hummed in her throat. "Now look to yo' lef'. Tell Queen what you see." She waited for him. "Gotta be somep'n. You try reel hard." But he shook his head.

"What you see ahead?"

He closed his eyes. "I see a door. A child by the door. He has a little toy car in his hand. He is runnin' the car up the wall by the door."

"What you hear?"

"I hear the train runnin' over a trestle."

"What you see in de back?"

"I didn't look behind."

"You got eyes now in de back a yo' head. You tell Queen now what you see in de back."

He began to laugh. But deep in himself he was yearning backward. He was finding a shadow and then the image that made the shadow.

"You tell Queen now."

"I see a man comin' through the door. With a bag, a satchel, some sort, in his hand."

"Where he gone?" she said. He shook his head. "He gotta be somewhere. Don' jes' disappear in de air."

He shook his head. She began to croon. She picked up the pail, took a drink of the brew, and gave the pail to Estes.

Seeing the boy drink, Caan suddenly roused. "My wife just disappeared in the air."

She crooned again. "What you see to de lef'?" she abruptly said.

He paused in his dream. "I see the man."

"Dat very same man? You tell me what dat man is like."

He shook his head. "I went to sleep."

"How come you gone to sleep you reckon?"

He stood up slowly. He fished in his pocket. "What I owe you, Queen?"

"I ast how come you gone to sleep."

He fumbled with bills. She sounded angry. "You don' owe nuttin' till you tell Queen dis: After you wake up and miss yo' wife . . . she ain' to de rat. Now look to de lef'."

He stared at her with a slow unease. "He isn't there."

She creased her lips. Her brown eyes snapped. "You owe Queen two dollah . . . Dat man to de lef' could make it t'ree."

He gave her five. She folded it over, put it to her lips, and stuffed it deep in her apron pocket. "Dat's mighty nice. You set fo' a spell. Queen gon' bring you a bite to eat." She turned to Estes, who lay on the ground with his feet on the tree. "You follow me, boy. I got work fo' you. An' bring dat pail."

Caan looked at his watch. It was after two. He sat in a mindless trance in the sun with his eyes on the cup they had left in the dirt. He was back in the train. To his left was the man across the aisle. His jacket was tan. With an effort of will Caan studied the face. It was thirty or so with an angular line. And the hair. He could not see the hair. He closed his eyes. Then he saw the hair, the color of sand. On the hand that hung from the arm of his seat Caan could see a ring. The ring was clouded and indistinct. But he felt the weight of it on the hand, somehow as if the hand were his own.

Then Estes was back with a plate of food. Caan ate it with hunger and a deep relief. The greens, the cornbread, and three warm biscuits with a strip of salt pork inside each one. He ate for his hunger, which seemed to be something apart from himself, and he ate for Tess. Estes sat, legs crossed, on the ground at his feet and filled the tin cup with dirt to the rim. Caan finished and gave the plate to him. "You thank your granny for me, you hear."

He stood up and walked back into the field. He waded deep in his weariness. With the sun at his back, he walked in his shadow. He began to sense that someone was following. The sense was so strong that twice he turned with a wild impression that Tess would be there in the hollow of the road or the willows beside it, about to call out, "Ben, wait for me." Once he heard her steps but, cursing the spell of the brew he had drunk, though it cost him an effort he would not turn. The train was screaming through Starwood country. He walked in his shadow behind the train.

When he got to town he stopped at the police station. Bailey sat at his desk. He was smoking a cigar. He looked up at Caan. "Yer wife ain' anywheres aroun' here, Caan. If she got off here she got back on and then she got off again someplace else."

"Help me," said Caan. "Just do what you can."

"I don' have the least idear what to do. I done call the state troopers. I done call the sheriff. I done call 'em again since you was last here. My advice is go home. Wait there for yer wife to git in touch. She wouldn't rightly know you was here, now, would she? Starwood ain' the first place would come to 'er mind. It ain' the first place come to nobody's mind. 'Less a course it's home."

In his weariness Caan held to the door. "She got off here. I ask you, how can I leave her here?"

"She ain' here, man! This town an' ever wheres aroun' this town knows about yer wife an' nobody seen 'er. A stranger is hard to miss aroun' here."

The train that went home had gone for the day, so he stayed in Starwood another night. Edith called at six. There was nothing to say.

In the bed he lay and waited for sleep. Then just as it came he was in the train moving back into sleep when she left him there. And Queen was saying, "I ast how come you gone to sleep?" He was shaking his head. But now the question lay deep in his flesh. Why had he been sleeping when he had slept well the night before?

The train was hurtling again through Starwood. He heard its cry. He almost heard the stammer of rails. He could see their sheen in the giant eye. And then it was thunder-deep in the hills.

And then like a dream, though he was waking, Tess was coming with paper cups, one in each of her small brown hands, and between her eyes the trace of a frown to keep them steady against the motion. She handed him one and stepped across. "Cream soda," she said. "We have to share. It was all they had. I poured it out 'cause you hate a bottle." Then she sipped her own and watched him drink.

He must have drifted into sleep at once. He seemed to remember the color of his sleep, how brown it was, and growing browner, but now and then punctured with a light and a sound. He thought it was strange how sharp and vivid his sleep became and yet how much like a dream it was when he was awake and she came with the cups. Why was this so? He turned in bed to erase the scene. Her figure in the aisle holding out the cup began to shimmer and then to fail and he let it go. He feared to fall into the sleep of the train. There was something about the sleep in the train — was it the motion or the sound of the rails? — that was different from any sleep he had known.

In the night he heard her outside in the court, the sound of her tears and the brush of her fingers across the door, then the soft, steady blow of a child that knocks with the palm of its hand. He wove the pain of it into his sleep and woke to hear how the sound had gathered force as he slept.

He opened his eyes into morning light. He roused and listened to the hammering beat, then staggered to the door and flung it open to find Titus outside, his hair like a torch in the early sun. "What is it?" Caan cried and braced himself for the joy or despair.

"I reckon yer surprised to see me, sir. I'm surprised myself to be standin' here." He was wearing jeans and red canvas shoes without laces.

Caan waited, speechless, still dazed with sleep.

"I reelize, sir, that I'm off the case. You made it mighty clear to me yestidy noon . . . But when I drop a case it don't jus' cut itself off in my mind. My mind keeps workin'. You understand me, sir?"

"What is it, Titus?"

"Word is got aroun' that yer leavin' Starwood, but 'fore you go I got somep'n to show you might be of interest."

Caan dressed at once. The boy was flexed with the weight of the mystery. "It's out a different road, not the one we took."

"Just tell me, Titus. Is it good or bad?"

"Sir, I don't consider it one way or other. In my opinion it is neutral-like. A clue in my opinion is nothin' but neutral."

They walked downhill through pine-studded land on a road that had once been graded and graveled but now was eroding into the willows that grew from the gullies on either side. Geese flying south were full of clamor.

They rounded a curve and abruptly below them a farmhouse was visible. In the sky above it a hawk was circling. Titus stopped and pointed.

"You see all that stuff growin' out to the side. Them vines is the kind that grapes grow on. They got grapes on 'em now."

Caan came at once to life. "Who lives there, Titus?"

"Man name a Ramer. Ain't from aroun' here."

"Are those the ones . . . are those the grapes my wife got off to buy?"

Titus looked away. He said with dignity: "Sir, I don't rightly know. I was took off the case. You may recall that, sir."

Caan nodded soberly. "I make a lot of mistakes."

"You could take it from here. I consider it a clue." He moistened a finger and smoothed his sideburns. "Sir, I'm obliged to point it out . . . take this road, about a mile from here there's a cave where several people been lost. 'Bout the onliest case I reely lost was a drunk man wandered into this cave . . ."

Caan broke it off. "She wouldn't be in there. My wife," he said, "is afraid of caves."

"If you say so, sir. And now I'll leave you. I'm reely not on duty today."

"I'm obliged to you, Titus."

Still he could not leave. He kicked at the gravel with a laceless shoe. "I could say this, sir. I reely appreciate yer position. Two year ago I had me a girl. We was reely close. You understand me, sir. She moved out a the state and never wrote ner nothin'. It was like the world reach out an' ate 'er up. I taken it hard."

Caan held out his hand. Titus shook it gravely. "A woman is alweez a problem, sir. I see it reel often in my line a work."

He was leaping a gully and off through the fields.

Caan turned and walked quickly to the dwelling below. It was a white frame house with a trim of red brick, surrounded by fields of corn and hay and a tidy planting of seedling pines. A little beyond lay an unpainted barn and several sheds, behind it a vineyard of half an acre. The house was the single dwelling in sight. He walked down the gravel road to the front. He could not suppress his agitation. He climbed the steps to the brick-railed porch and crossed and knocked at once on the door.

Sparrows were quarreling under the eaves. He watched a lizard inside the screen. He was about to leave to explore the vineyard when the door was opened and Queen stood before him. He was jolted to see her. And while he stood in the shock of her presence he built his defense lest again she enter his private world. And at once he wanted to search her face, her mind, whatever it was, whatever it took.

She gave no sign of being surprised. "Good mo'nin' to you, Mistah Caan."

Before her tall, dark self-possession he must wait a little before he spoke. "I wanted a word with Mr. Ramer."

She scanned the field before the house with her eyes heavy-lidded and brown as nuts. "He ain' here now. He done gone off on a trip somewheres."

A smell of cooking was in the air—bacon, coffee, something sweet. "You work here, Queen?"

"I cooks fo' him since his wife died t'ree fo' year ago. Can I git you some coffee, Mistah Caan?"

He did not like to take the fare of a man he had never met before. But he hungered for a reason he could not name to enter the house and know what it held.

He followed her into a paneled room with a fireplace in a wall of brick. She left him then. He could hear the sound of running water and presently the high-pitched bark of dogs. Against one wall stood a tall bronzed harp. And just beside it on a small pine chest a picture, leather framed, of a man and a woman standing together. He crossed the room to examine it. The color snapshot had been enlarged. He carried it to the window light. The man had his arm about the woman. His smile was broad. Caan was stunned to be facing the man of the train who had entered and sat across the aisle, the man Queen had summoned from the dark of his brain. Caan knew at once why the face had eluded his memory. With the colorless eyes and sandy hair there was nothing about him to catch in the mind. One hand held the woman's head to his. Caan could not take his eyes from the ring, which under the spell of Queen or the tea he had searched his memory and struggled to see. And now he saw the ring of the train, a glint of silver with a turquoise stone, the kind that is sold all over the West. The face of the woman was buried in flowers, as if she were smelling the blossoms she held. But the crown of her small dark head could be seen. It was wreathed in a braid of shining hair. He gazed at it with his heart in his throat and his eyes beginning to mist with pain.

Queen was back with a coffee tray. Her apron brushed the strings of the harp. "Is this his wife?" he said to her.

Queen glanced at the girl and turned away. "I reckon it be."

She left him there. The smell of the coffee sickened him. He placed the picture back on the chest. Across his mind swept the words of the day before with Titus. "My wife has never been here before." "You sure a that, sir?" He suddenly reeled with doubts half formed and shadow fears. The dogs began to bark in the yard with short, staccato, warning cries. In Starwood everything came with an echo. Tess . . . Tess and the woman here, her dark and shining crown of hair. The banjo she used to stroke and pluck with the sound of the harp that stood at his side. The Western ring on the hand before him . . . the postal from Phoenix that came for Tess. Queen with his tea . . . and the cup on the train he had drunk for Tess. And beyond this house the vines with grapes . . . and her voice in his ear, "I'll get you one. Ben, I'll be back." And cutting across like the sharpest echo the hum of the train and its lament, timed and pitched to the bay of the hounds. He turned to listen, yearning after it into the hills.

He crossed the room to the kitchen door. "Can you tell me what day he left on his trip?" She shook her head. "Can you tell me what his wife was like?"

She challenged him with her nut-brown eyes. "White folks looks all the same to me."

All the craziness of his loss and search, all the shift and check and evasion of Starwood, was tangled and trapped in the glance between them. He recalled her dry, overriding voice: "You tell Queen, now . . ." He wanted to force the dark memory tea through her own straight lips, to tell her she had eyes in the back of her head. But she stood before him, frail as a yellowing leaf with her grayed hair braided and coiled to her head and her dark mind coiled against his thrust. She was proud of her power, her hard-won sway over black and white, over rich and poor, over young and old. She asked the questions. She gave no answers.

She stood by the sink with steam from it wreathing her face in mist. He called through the mist. "Does my wife have somethin' to do with this house?"

She straightened and brushed her hands on her chest. "Yo' wife got nothin' to do wid dis town."

He was pleading now. "She got off here. She's got everything to do with this town."

And then Queen struck him down with her words. "You listen to Queen. Dis here is yo' las' stop, Mistah Caan. You makin' dis house take all dat blame you been holdin' in . . . An' you done tranced yo'se'f to do it." She turned to the sink and her voice ran low with the running water. "I knows when a man done tranced hisse'f. Time I laid my eyes on you I seed you's a man could trance hisse'f."

How could he know if she spoke the truth?

Back at the court he rang up Bailey. "We need to talk."

There was heavy silence. As if the wound had become his own, he knew Bailey fingered the patch on his head. "You referrin' to Ramer? Titus tol' me about it."

"Could his wife have died?"

"He said she died. Let's say she lef' here and never come back. But I reely ain' got the facts a the case. An' nobody here got the facts a the case." After another moment he said, "You through with me, Caan?"

"I'll never be through till I find my wife!"

He hung up the phone. The room was stifling, as if he had breathed up all its air and all the air that belonged to Starwood. Every road had a fork in it. He was getting lost with the sun going down. Something in Starwood broke truth into pieces and left him with shapes he could make nothing of. If he stayed it would all dissolve in the dark. Even his life with Tess would dissolve.

Then because nothing must be left undone, he dialed the number that was etched on his chain and listened to the ring in his empty house.

He took the train home in the afternoon. It was like unweaving their life together. When he got to Nashville and reached for his bag it was like unraveling their boarding the train. And back at the house he opened the bag to put away his clothes, and there were hers to be put away.

Always he lived in a state of listening. He listened in his sleep for the phone to ring. Away from the house he seemed to hear it. He listened for the sound of her knock on the door. At times he would hear it and go to look. And often in the wind he would know her voice. The chatter of squirrels, the bay of a hound, the call of a quail would become her voice. In his dreams at night he would sleep with her.

Sometimes when he walked in his open fields it seemed for a moment he walked near Starwood. He would look at the land with a seeking glance and know he was searching Starwood country. Slowly her presence came to haunt his land. It roamed the fields and lay deep in the hollows. He had loved his land. But now he saw it as if through tears.

There were things that had to be done for the winter. He hired a boy to help for a week. Some timbers of the barn must be replaced. The hay must be brought from the field and stored. The twelve bee hives must be winterized. He made cleats of wood to narrow the openings, and the work with them now was bittersweet. Tess had always been there to watch. And when he had robbed them deep in the summer, when he put on the veil like a bride of summer, she had watched him, troubled, with a frown on her face. "You don't look like yourself. Ben, you look so strange." So he took off the veil and with a smile put it over her head.

She removed it quickly. "It makes me afraid. It's like I was in a cave," she said. She stood far back. She was ready to run. "Be careful!" she called. And she covered her eyes when the bees drugged with smoke crawled over his veil.

But the honey she loved. She ate it on bread. She ate it at meals and in between. And she filled the jars that he took into town. She drew a star in the corner of each label. He asked what it meant. "It means I love the man that made this honey."

Edith came to visit. She watched him work and she cooked for him. She made pies of the apples behind the barn and put up some in the jars she found. She mended his clothes. She made some curtains to hang in the kitchen. She had no machine, so she sewed by hand. She kept saying, "I wish I had my Singer . . ."

It was hard for them both. He would see in her eyes that she thought of Joey when she saw in his own the loss of Tess. When it came time, she looked away from his face with tears. "I hate to leave you alone for the winter. Come stay with us. Hicks would love to have you. He needs a man around."

He smiled and shrugged. "And tell the cows where to find the hay?"

"You could," she said. "But you won't because you're waitin' for her. You think she's comin' back any time." She wiped her eyes.

He would not look at her when he said, "It's not like Joey."

"You could leave word where she was to call."

"She's alive," he said. "I'm closer to her than I've ever been. Would I feel that way if she wasn't alive?"

"Maybe so . . . maybe so. But what good is it, Ben? You're still a young man. You can't live your life bein' close to a woman who isn't here."

"Who's not comin' back. That's what you mean."

"Oh, Ben! Don't hate me. How can I know? How can you know?" She blew her nose. "Sometimes I feel like you was the one was lost in Starwood." She turned away. "Give it up, Ben."

"Give what up?" His eyes were hostile.

She cried a little and then she was gone. He was glad of it. He wanted to be alone to meet his loss, whatever kind it was, and then weave it into his house, his life.

When winter came on and the nights were long, more and more he was back in Starwood. He was roaming the land and searching for clues, recalling things that were said and done. Something he might have missed at the time. The roads—there were three—that he had not taken, he walked them now. With an effort of will he rehearsed events in precisely the order they had come to pass. And when he would come to the final day when Titus had led him down the road and left him standing beside the grapes, his throat would be full, his mind would stop. And then he would start all over again. The conductor's call, her talk of grapes . . .

The earth became for him Starwood swelled to a giant maze where his crippled mind sought her by day and night. He asked to know only where she was, not how or why. If he only knew where he would yield the rest.

And yet he could not yield the rest. A part of him searched the giant maze, but a part of him caught in its tangle of ways and his flesh was torn when he tried to flee: Was she forced? Did she go of her own sweet will? Was she lost to him to be found elsewhere? He could not endure his shifting mind. It was, in a way, like standing between the cars of the train after he woke to find her gone and bracing himself for the drift of the metal plates beneath. She was lost to him now, and lost perhaps for the rest of his days. But until he could stop the shift of his mind she was lost to his past. He was left with dust.

He stroked the chain she had placed on his wrist, and then one day he took it off. He kissed it and put it away for good. For perhaps it had only been in a dream that she was to claim him and fetch him home. I'm lost, he said. God knows I'm lost.

A neighbor of his owned a stretch of wood and had offered him hunting and firewood. Sometimes he came upon little wild grapes that were dried on the vine. Once he shot a young rabbit. He found blood on the ground and tracked it across a stretch of brown field and into the wood, and there it was blood on the fallen leaves and blood on the points of the winter fern. At length he was walking along a streambed, chill and damp where the frost had melted, and in between rocks that were etched with lichen and narrowed to a crevice where he lost the trail. He stood before the opening into the rocks. The cry of his hound was deep in the wood. And suddenly he had reached the end of the hunt. He was back in Starwood on the final road. Up ahead was the cave.

He threw down his gun and began to weep, without understanding, only knowing at first that ahead was the cave. Then wiping his eyes on the sleeve of his jacket he picked up his gun and called to his hound and returned to his fields. The house inside was dusk and cold. In muddied boots and heavy clothes he sat down before the fireless hearth. His hound was whimpering out in the yard. He was back with Bailey and the dog that whined on the floor of the station. "You sayin' she's in Starwood?" "She's got to be."

But he thrust himself now even further back. Back to the child that was left in the cave, to the girl who said she was drawn to caves, to the woman who lost herself in time, who always forgot what time it was . . . who lived in cave time, which was no time at all.

But how did she know of the cave in Starwood? There must have been a sign on the wall of the station, one he had not seen. Or something perhaps she had overheard. Did she ask the way? Did she say, "How far is it to the cave?" Was it possible that she could forget the train, his love, and the nights, and the mornings they rose, and the summers . . . oh, the summers of honey and bees, and the sparrows she talked to, and the rain on the roof?

For a little time she must have forgot and wandered deeper into the dark, till beside a stream she drank and slept . . . No, that was Joey.

But that was Tess.

He turned his face from the why and the how . . . the reason or madness . . . lest it bend his gaze from the sleep in the cave, where the iron band about his heart was burst at last and he was free. He did not want to go back again, to find the child asleep in the cave. He had found her once and had let her return.

Edith called up one evening late. "I couldn't sleep, Ben. You got it settled yet?"

"Yes, I got it settled."

"Don't tell me," she said. "Oh, Ben . . . I'm glad."

Tess dreamt in the cave where forever she slept. He lived in her dream, as it came to seem he always had. Now in the cold months she dreamt his winter life. If he happened to catch a glimpse of his face in a mirror frosted with the cloud of his breath, he could tell from his eyes that he walked in her dream, and he wanted to walk there and nowhere else.

But then when spring came, without knowing how, he woke from her dream. He took up her life where she had left it in Starwood. He lived it for her. The rain on the roof was the way she heard it. He talked to the sparrows. He tasted honey. He lived in cave time.

For a week in the summer he stayed with Edith. Hicks found him a job on a five-acre farm. But he didn't take it or try to explain. Edith watched him with eyes that knew his thought. And one day after

Hicks had gone to work, she told him, "Ben, go home. It's what you want." He kissed her and left.

Again he was living a summer for Tess. But in winter he found himself back in her dream. From her life in his own to his life in her dream and back again . . . it became a rhythm that pulsed with the beat of the changing year. And he dwelt in the grace of the years they had shared.

Four years passed. That fall he was in Atlanta with Edith. She had sent him downtown with a list of things. Hicks was not well. She hardly left the house.

It was warm for October and the streets were full. Some ten feet ahead a couple was walking, then waiting on the curb for the light to change. Under each of his arms the man carried a package. It gave him a little the look of wings. Perhaps it was why Caan had noticed him. And suddenly the woman beside him called out, "There's a man up there. He's going to fall!" A note in her voice had struck at his life.

The milling crowd looked high in the air at the man precariously perched on the ledge. He stood encaved in the dormer window, half held in its shadow, his head thrust into the autumn light.

Caan pressed to catch a glimpse of her form. It was small as a girl's. And the hair was dark and circled her head. It was not so dark, yet the sun was bright.

"Somebody make him go back," she said, and the voice was lighter and yet it was like.

Was it the shape, the cave of the window that drew him and held him above the crowd, perilously one with the man on the ledge, hearing the words as made for them both? She lifted her hand till the sleeve was falling away from her arm. In a moment a coral chain of a scar perhaps would coil below the wrist . . .

He turned and lost himself in the crowd. He had left her in Starwood.

ILLINOIS SHORT FICTION

Sho**r** **Story** Index